SOLE SURVIVOR

SOLE SURVIVOR

by

David Forster

Dales Large Print Books
Long Preston, North Yorkshire,
BD23 4ND, England.

British Library Cataloguing in Publication Data.

Forster, David
    Sole survivor.

    A catalogue record of this book is
    available from the British Library

    ISBN   1-84262-268-4 pbk

Cover illustration © Prieto by arrangement with
Norma Editorial S.A.

Published in Large Print 2003 by arrangement with
Robert Hale Ltd.

Dales Large Print is an imprint of Library Magna Books Ltd.

Printed and bound in Great Britain by
T.J. (International) Ltd., Cornwall, PL28 8RW

1

THE RENEGADES

There was a deadly calm in the valley around high noon on that summer day and all of it seemed to be focused on Steve Yarborough. At the southern end of the valley where the trail forked, one branch heading due west into the alkaline wastes of the desert which stretched clear to the state frontier and the other an old Indian trail leading into the hills, stood Freeman City. A sprawling collection of shanties, wooden-fronted stores, a livery stable, sheriff's office, and six saloons, it contained nothing worthy of its name.

For the wagon train heading west, it was just another trail town in a weary succession of such places. Ten years from now, thought Steve, as he sat easily in the saddle, wiping the sweat-caked dust from his face, those who rode with the train who were still alive would not even remember the name of the place.

He rode slowly along the dry, dusty street that shimmered in the noon heat, aware of the curious glances of the men who lounged on the wooden boardwalks and the red-lipped women on the veranda of one of the saloons. A tall, sandy-haired, silent man with strange, snapping eyes which told of things a man learns only in war. He wore the heavy Colts low, ready to leap into his hands like living things.

The Conestoga wagons, seven of them, stood on the edge of Freeman City, two with fresh red paint glistening in the sun. There was the smell of meat cooking and the heavy aroma of coffee in the air as he rode between two of the wagons and reined the sorrel, staring down at the largest man he had ever seen in his life.

'You made up yore mind yet, Madison?' he asked softly. 'Do I get to join the train when you pull out tonight?'

The other sucked in thick lips, speared a hunk of roast meat on the long-bladed knife and tore at it avidly with strong, pointed teeth. He wiped the back of his hand across the thick, luxuriant growth of the red beard. He chewed reflectively for a moment, staring off into the shimmering, heat-hazed distance, then nodded slowly. 'You look to me like a wild man, Yarborough. A handy man with those guns of yores. A dangerous man to have on the trip with us, or a good man. I'm not shore which at the moment, but I figger you can come along.' His eyes roamed towards the heavy, double-barrelled rifle which leaned against the wheel of the Conestoga wagon nearby. 'One wrong move, though, and you'll be a dead man.'

'Thanks.' Yarborough shucked back the brim of the wide hat and rubbed the sweat from his brow. The clear grey eyes wandered over the waiting wagons, taking in everything; the children playing noisily around the rear of the last wagon in the line where two of the cows had been hitched to the back, the silent women, mostly dressed in their sombre poke-bonnets, the grim-faced men with their determined expressions, with their eyes which always seemed to be moving, to be looking far beyond the horizon, to the green, stretching lands of California. The rich, red gold had been recently discovered there and even now, wagon trains were heading west over the barren, inhospitable country, each man striving to get there to reap his fortune in a virgin country.

As he unsaddled the sorrel and allowed it

to drink its fill, he fell to wondering about Madison. There was something strange and different about this giant of a man with the flaming red beard and the hair to match. He guessed that behind the other there lay more than a score of years – harsh, bitter years filled with conflict and hard times. Many days of personal defeat and few of victory.

The wagon train moved out that evening. The horses set in the traces of the wagons pulled strongly as they reached the fork in the trail and took the wide branch leading into the desert. A hundred yards. Two hundred. The wheels creaked and rattled on the thick, wooden axles, the ground beneath them soft and treacherous, dry and yellow. Steve Yarborough sat tall in the saddle, riding a little ahead of the train. On the other side of the wide trail, Madison rode a black stallion. The thick brows jutted forward, drawn bar-straight over the forbidding eyes.

It had been Madison's idea to move out in the evening, when the heat of day had passed. They could make good time and he was anxious to be on his way as soon as possible. There was something deep driving this man, something hard and ruthless which gave him no rest. It was easy now. As yet, the country was little different to that which they had travelled for a hundred miles. But it would soon change. The country, nature, everything would be against them. The long, scorching days of thirst lay just ahead and they were riding towards them as quickly as they could go.

They did not pause until they reached the western end of the Condon fault where it looked down upon the narrow bend of the Leon River. Beneath the wheels of the heavy wagons, the earth gave way to shifting sand, and ahead of them, now that it was almost dawn, they could make out the whiter haze which marked the beginning of the great alkaline wastes of the desert which stretched ahead of the team for close on fifty miles. There would be no grazing for the small herd of cattle which they had brought with them. The animals would have to drink their fill at the river and make that last them until they pushed through, clear to the other side of the wilderness. By screwing up his eyes against the searing glare of sunlight striking the desert, Yarborough could just make out the rising peaks of the mountains on the far horizon.

Slowly, the creaking wagons were turned until they lay along the nearer bank of the sluggish river. The horses were unhitched and the women made a meal over the brush fires which were lit among the wagons. Yarborough slipped the saddle off the sorrel and walked back up the dry, sandy slope to where Madison sat cross-legged on the ground a couple of feet from the fire. He sat down opposite him.

'You figure on lying up here today and then heading out in the evening, Madison?' he asked, helping himself to the food in the pan where it sizzled over the fire.

'See anything wrong in that idea?' grunted the other, the huge, leonine head hunched forward on the wide shoulders.

'Nope.' Yarborough shook his head slowly. 'I reckon you're right. Travelling by night means we can rest up during the heat of the day and it probably makes for safer riding.'

No movement by the other man. No immediate comment. But the eyes lifted and found Yarborough's, clung interrogatively for a moment. There was a question in them. Finally, Madison said harshly: 'You travelled these parts before?'

'Could be. That's bad country up ahead. Mile after mile of empty wilderness. It's easy for a man to lose himself there, and easier for him to die.'

'We'll make it,' growled the other thickly. He chewed on his food, drank deeply of the hot coffee. One booted foot swept out and kicked the embers into fresh life. 'I've ridden over worse territory than this.'

'With a wagon train?' Yarborough arched his brows. He turned away for a moment and glanced along the line. Inwardly, he wondered how many of these people could even guess at what they were letting themselves in for, riding with this man, trusting themselves to him. None of them would have asked any questions. But out here in the frontier west, questions were seldom asked. Provided a man promised to take you through the bad country and on to California, you fell in with him: guides were few, most of the men having moved on ahead to the rich gold fields.

'I'll get them through,' said the other harshly. He looked again towards the west, to the far bank of the river as if debating whether to cross over into the desert before they rested up, or wait until nightfall before moving the tired horses again.

'You ain't scared of the talk we heard back there in Freeman City?' Steve lifted the coal-black brows just a fraction and the clear grey eyes held the other's. Slowly and

15

reluctantly, Madison shook the huge head. He looked at Steve with eyes that seemed to be focused on infinity.

'You mean that wild talk of renegade outlaws in this part of the territory? That was nothing more than the usual talk you get in these parts. Could be a stage gets held up once in a while and before you know it, the whole country is sparked off into a hunt.' The words were flat in the stillness. Far off, down by the bank of the Leon, a handful of men were watering the cattle which had moved with them during the long pull out of town.

'If I were you,' said Steve, choosing his words carefully, 'I'd listen to some of that talk. I heard more than you did. You seemed to spend all of your time with the train, outside Freeman City. I went in and had a talk with the sheriff there. Seems these people do have something to be scared about. The last wagon train which headed out this way, five months ago, never made it. They got into the desert about twenty miles over the river there – and that was the end for them all. Three days later, a party found the ashes where the train had been fired, the bodies of those who were with it, no horses, no belongings that were worth thieving. And what's more to the point – no survivors.'

'I heard something about that,' acknowledged the other grudgingly. 'I don't set no store on it. Besides, if we run into that bunch of outlaws on this trip, we've enough here to fight them off. Close on twenty men with guns and ammunition and you're pretty handy with your gun.'

'You reckon those other men will know how to handle a gun if we're attacked?'

'They'll use their guns,' muttered Madison emphatically, 'or they'll die. When the choice is put in front of them, they'll know what to do. I've seen craven cowards turned into heroes within minutes under fire.'

Steve pulled the plateful of food towards him and began to eat. Madison pushed himself on to his feet, went out to the cookpot and dipped his fingers into the boiling water. For a moment, the muscles of his face tightened and then he withdrew his hand, a hunk of beef between finger and thumb. He thrust it into his mouth and chewed reflectively on it for a long moment before swallowing. Looking down from his tremendous height, he said softly: 'I'm depending upon you, Yarborough, not to spread any word of what you heard in Freeman City among the others on this

17

train. There's no point in starting any panic when there may be no need. We'll keep a sharp eye open for trouble, ready to spot it before it comes – you and I. Agreed?'

Slowly, Steve drained the cup of coffee, pondered for a moment, then nodded with an equal slowness. 'Very well, if that's the way you want it, Madison. But I still reckon that we're heading into trouble out there, big trouble.' He heaved himself to his feet, checked the Colts in his holsters. There was no wasted movement about anything that this tall, lean-faced man did.

Most of them slept through the terrible heat of the day, a shimmering, flesh-drying heat which probed into the wagons and made their sleep uneasy. The cows bellowed feebly through the long afternoon. A few of the children played a little listlessly by the bank of the river, but as the heat of high noon came, they too, made their way into the wagons, eyes tender and smarting from the brilliant, searing glare of the white desert beyond the river.

Come nightfall and they were on the move once more, fording the river, urging the horses through the water which, at its deepest, was less than two feet to the bottom. One after the other, the wagons climbed the far bank and started out into the desert which stretched away clear to the distant mountains. Now that the sun had gone down, the wind had a raw edge to it. The desert lost its heat quickly with the setting of the sun and cold closed like a thick, tight blanket around them. Steve Yarborough took up his usual position a little ahead of the lead wagon, eyes probing the darkness which lay all around them, the creaking of the wagons sounding un-naturally loud in his ears. Surely, his mind warned him, every renegade in the area would be able to hear those wagons on the move. It was not that he was afraid for himself. Many times in the past, he has been forced to fight in order to stay alive. But there were women and children with this wagon train. He did not want to see them slaughtered by gunslingers who knew no mercy.

Madison wheeled his mount suddenly and rode over until he was alongside Steve. He said quietly, 'I reckon it might be wise if you were to ride on ahead a little way, scout out the area. Just to be safe.'

Steve nodded slowly. Touching spurs to the sorrel, he felt the animal bound forward, ears flattened back against its head. A mile from the train, he reined the mount, rode more slowly now, eyes and ears alert for trouble. Silence seemed to have fallen over the ground around him. Above him lay the Texas moon, floating smoothly in a cloudless sky – hard, round and cold. It threw a strange grey light over the desert, giving everything a peculiarly monochrome appearance. From somewhere in the distance up ahead, a coyote wailed a dismal dirge to the moon, the weird, hacking cry sending a little shiver along his spine as he sat the saddle easily. In that single sound lay all of the danger, the cruelty and the death which made up the desert.

He rode westward for the best part of an hour, was on the point of reining the sorrel and starting back for the train when the smell of wood smoke reached his nostrils. It hung on the still air like a threat as he turned the sorrel and edged to his right. Here, rough boulders thrust themselves up from the flatness of the desert and his horse picked its way carefully among them. He came across the remains of the fire less than five minutes later and sat tensed in the saddle, staring down towards it, clearly visible in the grey moonlight.

The fire had burned low and sand had

been tossed on to it, hurriedly, so that it had not been completely extinguished and a little of the wood still smouldered. Around it, in the soft ground, were the hoofprints of many horses. His keen-eyed gaze took in every detail, and what he saw, brought the fear back into his mind with a rush. Slipping from the saddle, he examined the fire closely and then rose swiftly to his feet, satisfied. This fire had not been started by Indians but by white men; and to his mind, conditioned by what he had seen and heard back in Freeman City, that meant only one thing. Outlaws had been here, and only a little while earlier. Swiftly now, he climbed back into the saddle, urged the horse forward. Men did not light a fire out here in the middle of the desert and leave it in such a hurry unless they had something on their minds – something like murder and robbery. God alone knew where the outlaw band was at that very moment, possibly circling around to the east ready to attack as soon as they figured the time was ripe. He guessed there would be about a score of them and even as the thought passed through his mind, knew Madison and the other men in the wagon train had no chance whatever of holding them off if they did attack.

He spurred the sorrel forward, over a long, low ridge of treacherously shifting sand, down the far side and into the flat, featureless country once more. There came the rising, strangely undulant cry of a coyote, nearer than the first wail he had heard. Or was it the call of a coyote? Might it not be a signal from one of the outlaws to another? He half turned in the saddle and threw a swiftly, apprehensive glance in the direction from which the mournful wail had come, but even in the flooding moonlight there was nothing to be seen. A hundred men could be lying in wait out there and there would be no sign of them until they came in to attack.

Less than forty minutes later, he spotted the wagons, crossing the faint light of the desert where the moonlight continued to fall along the trail. They lumbered slowly forward, Madison just visible leading the way, head thrown well back on his shoulders. A man confident in his own strength, thought Steve tightly, but a man who deluded himself if he considered they would get across this terrible expanse of desert in one piece. Those outlaws were somewhere in the neighbourhood. Occasionally, as he rode forward, cutting diagonally across the desert so as to come up alongside the huge, red-bearded man, he could hear the sharp, urgent cries of the men who drove the Conestoga wagons. The womenfolk would probably be in the wagons, asleep; although some of these hard-featured women who knew how to handle a high-powered Lee Enfield rifle, would be seated on the buckboard beside their menfolk, ready to shoot if there was any kind of trouble.

Madison turned and eyed him curiously as he rode up. The thick lips parted in a faint smile. 'Find anything up ahead?'

'Plenty, and I like none of it,' he said grimly. 'There are renegades round here some place. I came across one of their fires. They'd kicked sand over it, but it was still smouldering. From the prints in the earth around it, I'd guess there were about a score of them. And they didn't hit out along the trail because they were scared of us. They're waiting to bushwhack us somewhere along the trail.'

'How can you be sure of that?' Apparently the big man was loath to halt the train just on the unsupported evidence of this one man. His object was to get them through, certainly across this burning, alkaline hell before too many days were allowed to pass.

It had been known for a wagon train to take a week to cross the fifty or sixty miles of desert and by the end of that time, half of the passengers were hovering on the edge of madness.

'I don't need to be sure of what I saw,' retorted Steve, half-angrily. 'There won't be anyone else out here in the desert, lighting fires just before we arrive on the scene. They've had us spotted since we left Freeman City. They probably know everything we're carrying with us.'

For a second, even in the faint moonlight, he felt certain that the big man's eyes narrowed a little. He experienced a faint sense of grim amusement, knowing the thoughts passing through Madison's mind at that moment.

He said tightly: 'They know about the gold you're carrying with you.'

Madison whirled on him sharply, half-lifting himself from the saddle. The dark eyes flashed brilliantly. 'What do you know of the gold?' he snarled. The heavy Colt was half-drawn from its leather scabbard, then thrust back again when Steve made no move towards his own guns.

'You're a fool, Madison, if you think it's such a big secret. I heard about that gold in the saloon in Freeman City. Seems everybody there knows about it, that is, everybody who oughtn't to know. Word like that travels swiftly in these frontier parts. They've had men out there in Freeman City ever since you arrived there, three days ago.' It was blunt speech, but this was a moment that required it. If they were to stand a chance of survival, he was certain they had very little time. Even before the other spoke, he was peering keenly around him, the wagon train lumbering forward twenty yards away along the wide, ragged trail. They would need to take up defensive positions. Had they been back near the river, they would have been able to make use of a natural defensive barrier. But the outlaws had evidently been biding their time, letting them get further from the river and Freeman City, before they attacked.

Madison was obviously still unconvinced. The desert was quiet around them, empty as far as the eye could see. No sign of danger. No indication that death might be lying in wait for them up ahead. Madison turned in the saddle and motioned to the first wagon. It creaked to a halt and the man seated on the buckboard climbed down and walked towards them as the other wagons slowed.

'Could be trouble up ahead, Jessup,' said Madison tightly. His face was quite expressionless. 'Yarborough has found a fire burning about a mile or so in front of us, a little way off the trail. Marks of plenty of horses there, too. It could be those outlaws we heard about back in town.'

Along the train, others in the wagons were stirring to wakefulness. Out of the corner of his eye, Steve noticed several of the women and children peering through the drapes.

'What do you reckon we ought to do, Madison?' asked Jessup hoarsely. 'It still wants four hours to dawn and in that time, we could move these wagons twenty miles or more and be halfway across this goddamned desert.'

Madison listened attentively. He nodded, jerked his thumb in the direction of the wagons. 'The others will like it better if we keep moving.' He turned to Steve. 'You saw nothing definite there, no sign of any riders on your way back to the train?'

'No.' Steve shook his head. 'But that ain't no reason for risking the lives of everybody on this train. You didn't expect them to show themselves until they were ready to attack, did you?'

Madison slid the heavy rifle from its

26

scabbard, checked it quietly, then gave a harsh laugh. 'We move on,' he said defiantly. 'If we run into trouble, we'll give better than we get.' As Jessup moved back to the waiting wagon, Madison called after him. 'Warn the others we may run into trouble, be ready to use their guns.' One heavy arm swung around to indicate the trail ahead and three minutes later, they moved on, the wagons creaking and rolling over the shifting sand. Soon they were moving quickly along the trail, the cold air swirling around them. A quarter mile, a half mile. Still no sign of trouble, although Steve's eyes roamed the trail ahead, never still. Silent, he sat the saddle uneasily now, expecting trouble, but not knowing when, nor from which direction it would come.

All he could hope, was that he could spot the outlaws while there was still time in which to form some swift plan of action. Turning his head, he glanced back towards the wagons. Now, he could see most of the women, up on the buckboards with their menfolk, some holding the rifles ready. Evidently, Jessup had passed the warning along the train. This was going to be an anxious night for all of them. A dozen women there, perhaps more. Women who knew what they were heading into when they had left the safety of the east, to come out here in search of gold and a new country.

The attack came! Steve had barely time in which to turn his head before the outlaws were on them. They had played them false, had not come from the desert which lay ahead of them, the direction from which they could have been expected, but had circled around them, come up on their rear. They were around the wagons before Steve was aware that they were there. A gun crashed and blazed in the pale moonlight. A second and third gave answer. Then more shots bucketed over the silence of the white desert.

All of this had happened in the short fraction of a second while Steve was twisting in the saddle.

His warning shout was ripped from his throat. 'Keep those wagons bunched.' Most of them heard the warning, for it was echoed by the bull-like voice which belonged to Madison. The big man reined his horse in front of one of the wagons, threw himself from the saddle with a speed surprising in a man of his tremendous bulk, landing on the buckboard, taking the rifle with him. Yarborough urged his horse back to the wagons, the guns slicking from leather as he rode in. Two outlaws rode past him, yelling savagely at the tops of their voices. Hard-faced, bearded men whose only law was to kill and rob. Both men swung past, then toppled from their saddles as the bullets struck home. Steve crowded them close, made sure they were dead, then eased his way back to the nearest wagon. A frightened-faced woman peered down at him in the dimness. The man beside her was lying against the post, blood a dark and ugly stain on his shirt. He held the smashed shoulder with the clawed fingers of his left hand, struggling to retain his hold on the reins with his right, as the two horses in the traces leapt forward, maddened by the shooting. These horses had not been bred for battle, shied at the slightest sound. He threw himself down as the wagon ground to a halt, the guns in his hands speaking death. No time in which to estimate how many outlaws there were. Time only to shoot and reload as quickly as possible, to shoot at dark figures which raced by on their swift mounts, to kill and run the risk of being killed.

High, hard, brittle voices yelled in the

darkness, shouting above the stabbing spits of orange flame. Clambering on to the wagon, Steve dragged the injured man back inside, turned to the white-featured woman who stared at him over the moaning body.

'See what you can do for him.' he snapped. 'Don't show yourself unless you have to. Those men out there are killers.'

He didn't need to tell her that, but there was the look of shock on her face and he wanted to be sure she would stay under cover. Back on the buckboard, he snapped a couple of quick shots into the darkness. Saw one of the fleeting shadows clutch at a shattered arm. Rifles were answering the gunfire now, as the men in the wagon train fought for their lives. It was going to be a grim and terrible fight, he reflected coolly, flinching as a bullet smacked into wood-work close to his head. Along the line, some of the women were firing and loading now. But the outlaws had brought more with them than guns. Steve saw the flash of flame out of the corner of his eye and cursed himself for not remembering what he had been told about the other wagon train that had been bushwhacked out here in the desert not so long before. The flaring torch touched the roof of a wagon near the end of the train. Seconds later, two more soared up into the pale moonlight as they were lit and tossed on to the canvas. Dry as tinder, every drop of moisture burned out of it by the scorching desert sun, the canvas caught the flames and burned furiously. Steve felt his throat go dry as he lay flat on his stomach and watched the silhouette of a woman as she tried desperately to smother the flames with water from the large wooden bucket, saw her back arch convulsively as two of the outlaws emptied their guns into her body as they rode past. She fell back with a loud cry and disappeared from sight. Moments later, the flames engulfed the wagon completely.

The hammers of his guns clicked on spent cartridges. There came a sudden shriek from the woman inside the wagon. He turned his head swiftly. The canvas here was already alight, blazing fiercely. Swiftly, he pulled the long-bladed knife from his belt, ripped and slashed at the canvas hoops on one side of the wagon until the ropes had been cut through, then in spite of the flames which burned at the backs of his hands, he tore the whole, blazing mass off with a surge of superhuman strength.

The outlaws came surging in again. This time, they moved in silently. There was no yelling, no harsh voices. Bullets hummed through the air around Steve as he worked desperately, loading shells into the chambers of the sixguns. There was a shot from the direction of the end of the wagon train, followed by a hoarse yell of pain and the sound of a heavy body falling to the ground. They were fighting a losing battle here. The outlaws still outnumbered them by almost two to one and they could strike without warning from any direction, riding in from the dark shadows of the desert. They had chosen the spot well, probably guessed that they would urge the horses to the utmost in an attempt to cover as much ground as possible before dawn.

He fired instinctively, drawing a bead on two men who swept by, their guns blazing. One man jerked back in the saddle as the bullet caught him, almost slid out of it, but somehow succeeded in hanging on with one hand. Steve drew in a deep breath, felt the smoky air go down into his lungs like fire. The heat from the burning canvas now lying on the sand by the side of the wagon struck him forcibly like a physical blow. There was no sign of Madison and he stared about him, blinking his eyes several times, as the smoke threatened to blind him, searching for the big man, knowing with a strange kind of instinct, that so long as the other remained alive, they had a chance; a very slender one, but a chance all the same.

A rifle barked harshly close at hand. Turning his head, he caught a fragmentary glimpse of the other, his huge bull-neck and shoulders clearly visible and unmistakable as he stood on the front of the next wagon. The next instant Madison had dropped the rifle and bent swiftly. There was a loose coil of rope in his hands when Steve could next see him, outlined against the flames creeping up the sides of the wagon. He spun it over the necks of the bucking, lurching horses, still in the traces, the fear showing in every outline of their bodies. The rope snapped tight as it fell over the shoulders of one of the men riding by and the outlaw was jerked from his mount and thrown heavily to the ground a couple of yards away, his body twisting once in the air before he was slammed against the earth. Arms pinioned to his sides, he sat there, clearly visible in the lurid red glow of the flames. Then something seemed to flash like a streak of quicksilver through the air, something which left Madison's right hand and finished its headlong flight a second later in the man's back between the shoulder blades, the hilt just visible.

Gradually, the firing from the wagon train began to die away. The men in the wagons were no match for gunslingers like these. Only Steve and Madison knew how to use a gun in anger. Crouching down, Steve waited for the outlaws to move in for the kill. They had either killed or wounded most of the men on the train and now knew that there was very little opposition left. But they were still cautious. Several of their number had been killed during the short, fierce battle and the rest were taking no chances. As he lay there, breathing heavily, staring out through the mist which blurred his smoke-filled eyes, Steve saw the small bunch of riders heading in from the south. The outlaw band had withdrawn a little way, to give the fire a chance to smoke any of the survivors out into the open, where they would make excellent targets for their guns. Now, they were not sure how many men were left alive, but they knew that it could not be many.

The man who rode in the lead was short and stocky, bareheaded, dressed in a black shirt, and under the mop of dark hair, his forehead was high and strangely white, like the belly of a fish, the small, porcine eyes staring out without feeling at the long train of burning wagons. Steve knew that he would remember that face for as long as he lived; and he swore that if he did live, this man would stand in front of his guns one day and pay for what he had done. He lifted his guns, fired twice at the approaching men, but the bullets went wide for none of them fell and the only reply was a sudden fusillade of bullets which smashed around the wagon. He leaned back to fire again, but the fingers on the triggers of the guns never moved. A bullet, scorching out of the darkness, ploughed a neat furrow along the side of his skull and he pitched forward over the smouldering side of the wagon as the blackness of unconsciousness swamped over him.

Once, twice, Steve struggled to the surface, to clutch at consciousness, only to slip back again into the darkness. How long he lay there, on the hot alkaline sand, it was impossible to tell. When he finally did regain consciousness long enough to look about him and to understand what he saw, it was light and the sun was past its zenith and dipping down towards the mountains on the western skyline. Blinking his eyes, he pushed himself on to his feet, stood for a long moment, looking about him at the

35

shambles of what had once been a wagon train. The massacre had been savage and complete. Nothing moved on the bitter waste of the desert wilderness. He put his hand up to his head to ease away some of the pain that throbbed and beat behind his temples. The blood was pounding through his veins and there was a thick, woolly feeling in his mouth and at the back of his throat. Smoke still hung dense and heavy in the air, mingled with the smell of smouldering wood. There was no sign of the outlaws. Evidently they had looted the wagons and left him for dead along with the others. Shuffling his feet in the sand, he made his way forward, found a water bottle still hanging on the back of one of the charred hulks, lifted it to his lips and drank deeply of the warm, brackish water in it, allowing it to trickle slowly down his throat.

Sweat beaded his forehead and trickled into his eyes, half-blinding him. The white, eye-searing glare from the sun-filled desert all around him did the rest. Drawing in a deep sobbing breath, he hunted through the wagons, ignoring the dead. Madison's body lay in one of the wagons, the rifle still clutched in his huge hands. The red beard jutted defiantly at the sky and even in death he looked big and dangerous.

There were no horses. Either the outlaws had cut them loose and taken them with them, or they had broken free of the traces, stampeding from the fire. Even if that was what had happened, they could be clear across the desert by now, he told himself. No point in trying to find them. All that he could do now, if he wanted to live, was to head for those hills on the horizon. He guessed that there were close on three hours of daylight left and then the cool night would come. For a moment, he stared out along the trail which stretched away in front of him, something which could just be distinguished from the surrounding desert, and his eyes glittered fiercely. He was still alive, wounded it was true, where the bullet had creased his skull, but he had something to live for now, something to drive him on across the burning hell of the desert. He had sworn to kill these men, especially that man whose face he had seen in the lurid red glow from the blazing wagons; and that was something he intended to do.

An early dusk saw him moving forward slowly along the trail, heading in the direction of the red glow in the western sky where the sun had gone down. Already the cold fingers of the night were closing about him and the wound on his skull, although it had now stopped bleeding and he had managed to wash it with water from one of the canteens, still pained him. His head throbbed violently and every step he took sent a tremor spilling along his legs.

There were moments during that night when he thought that he was not going to make it. He still had his guns and they were loaded, ready to kill, but he could hear the drumming of hoofs in the distance somewhere, behind him, and it came to him then that perhaps these men had gone back to that wagon train and had found that he was gone, that he had not been killed; and now they were tracking him down to kill him. Not that they would have much to fear from him, but he must surely have seen their faces, could identify them to a sheriff's posse if he got out of that desert alive. Because of his wounded condition, they possibly did not believe that he could get very far and they were moving in circles around the train. He tightened his lips convulsively and forced his flagging feet to continue to move, shuffling through the clinging sand which impeded his progress.

The hours passed slowly. Now he did not

seem weak so much as light-headed and he knew with a sick certainty that another sun must rise and make its way slowly across a burning heaven before he could reach the far side of the desert. And this time, there would be no wagon in which he could find shade. He was acutely aware of the water that swilled around inside the canteen he carried at his belt. Only half full now, there was little enough water to last him for this terrible journey and he had travelled this desert twice before and knew there were no waterholes along this devil's trail.

If only he could find one of the horses, he would stand a more than even chance. But on foot – he shook his head in an effort to clear it. Several times, he stumbled, clawed himself upright and forced himself to keep moving. Once he stopped, once he surrendered to the fatigue and weariness which dragged endlessly at his body, it would mean the end. The moon passed across the sky, the stars began to dim and there was a red flush in the sky at his back as the dawn began to brighten. He climbed a low, craggy ridge and stared about him through narrowed eyes. The edge of the desert still seemed to be as far off as ever. In front of him there was only the white expanse of the desert, offering him no shade, no place where he could rest and find shelter from the burning sun. As he stumbled forward his mind ran over the terrible events of the previous day. The disaster to the wagon train had come as a stunning surprise. He thought of the people who had been killed and the thought was enough to keep him moving.

2

WHITE WILDERNESS

At Steve's back, the sun was a ball of flame which hung in the heavens and poured its heat down on the burning sand of the desert, on the vast waste of alkali that went in every direction, so that it seemed to him that he was nothing more than a tiny speck of humanity in a shimmering sea of whiteness. His legs seemed to be moving slowly of their own volition and when he fell, which was often now, it was becoming increasingly difficult to get back on to his feet.

With high noon, he came to a deep rift which lay between two rising humps of ground. There was no shade here, but unable to continue any further, he threw himself on to the burning ground, buried his head in his elbows, and fell into an exhausted sleep. When he woke, the sun was closer to the western horizon and the nearer ridge had thrown a shadow over the ground. He lay in it, without being able to move, for

41

what seemed an eternity, until the great red ball of the sun touched the horizon. Bitterness rose in him as he forced himself upwards from the hot ground. His limbs were stiff and after taking another sip of water from the canteen, he found difficulty in forcing his legs to move again. His eyes seemed unable to focus properly and his vision was blurred.

The wound in his head was still paining him and the blood had congealed there and there was no water with which to clean it. Sand had worked its way into the folds of his skin, itching and irritating. The harsh alkali burned his throat and flesh, made every breath he took an individual torture. By the middle of the morning he could scarcely move. Ahead of him, a low ridge rose out of the desert and the trail lifted over it, vanishing in mystery over the other side. Slowly, agonizingly, he pulled his way up the ridge, stumbling with every step he took; half out of his mind, he reached the top and stared into the shimmering white distance, at the small waterhole less than fifty feet away on the far side of the ridge and the lone horse, head lowered, which stood there. It lumbered slowly away as he approached at a shuffling run. He threw himself down at the waterhole edge, splashing the muddy brackish water into his face, scooping it up in the palm of his hand and drinking greedily. Gradually, a little of the strength returned to his body. He filled the canteen, rose unsteadily to his feet and moved towards the horse. It shied away from him, uncertain. His limbs were still stiff, but he finally made it. There was a saddle on the horse and he swung himself up into it. Somewhat listlessly, he turned the animal and headed it away from the waterhole. What he needed most now was to set thirty or thirty-five miles between him and the wrecked wagon train. Then he would be able to rest a little while and tend to the wound in his head.

Keeping the horse at a steady lope, he lolled drunkenly in the saddle, hardly aware of anything that happened. Often, he dozed, scarcely conscious, with one eye open to keep the horse on a westward course. The mountains in the distance mocked him cruelly. Always, as the hours passed, the shimmering peaks seemed to be as far off as ever, never coming any closer. There was no thought of stopping, or of turning back to the waterhole. The one burning thought in his mind was to keep on going, to get to the green country, to carry out his vow of vengeance on the band that had bushwhacked the wagon train.

The long afternoon wore on. The sun blazed down on the rolling desert and the distant skyline wavered and blurred in front of him. The horse moved slowly now, the sound of its feet deadened by the shifting alkali. That evening, he was within reach of the foothills. Slipping from the saddle, he drank his fill from the canteen, leaving a little water for the next day.

The gnawing hunger pains in the pit of his stomach made it impossible for him to sleep that night, although a great weariness lay in his body and every muscle and fibre ached intolerably. Now that he was the sole survivor of that raid on the train, that fiendish bunch of outlaws would have to finish him off if they could, to prevent him from identifying and testifying against them. It would have been a simple matter for them to follow his trail in the desert, and there had been nothing to obliterate the tracks of his horse, tracks which could lead them out here.

Early the following morning, stiff and bruised, he got to his feet, allowed a mouthful of water to swill around his mouth, swallowing it reluctantly, then corked the canteen. Then he glanced up, blinking his eyes against the red glow in the east which heralded the rising sun. The closing-in riders resembled nothing more than a bunch of black specks far out in the desert, back along the way he had ridden the previous day. They were coming up fast, spurring their mounts cruelly, riding them to the limit. Obviously, they had thought to catch him unawares, while still asleep.

There was no time to be lost if he was to stay alive. He could not remain there and hope to outshoot that bunch. He hazarded a guess that there were close on a dozen men in the band and although he could not identify them for certain at that distance, he had no doubts as to who they were. The remnants of the band that had jumped the wagon train. As he had guessed they had picked up the trail of his horse, followed him easily in the moonlight, gaining ground rapidly. The shifting ground, dry and fine, effectively drowned any thunder of hoofs. They also approached him from the dawn, with the light of the morning sky at their backs.

Swiftly, he climbed up into the saddle, pulling the horse's head around harshly, digging in the rowelled spurs. Another two miles to go and he would be inside the timber country among the foothills. But although his mount had rested during the night, it had had no food and no water since they had left the waterhole the previous noon. It was almost beat and those would be fresh horses coming up behind him. A nauseating pain began low in the middle of his stomach as he crouched down over the horse's neck, head low, turning it towards the hills.

There was a wide river at the border of the desert, between it and the low foothills which lay beyond. He was forced to swim the horse here; there were no crossing places there and during the night, he had wandered off the trail a little. On the other side, he entered scrub country, huge boulders which thrust themselves up out of stony ground, making progress slow and difficult. Several times he threw swift glances over his shoulder at his pursuers. Now they were less than a mile behind, coming up fast. He reined up against a brush wall, shaded his eyes against the sun. The renegades put their horses to the river, swum them over at almost exactly the same point as he had crossed. Obviously, they were still following his trail in the soft sand.

Carefully, he checked the sixguns, made sure that every chamber showed the protruding, rounded end of a bullet, before thrusting them back into their holsters. Behind him, the ground rose steeply into the hills. Rugged ground over which it would be virtually impossible for him to ride with his mount in its present condition. Sweating profusely, it could carry him only a short distance further. Desperately, he cast about him, looking for a good defensive position. The realization came to him now that the showdown had come somewhat earlier than he had anticipated, that he would have to stand his ground and shoot it out with these men now. He could no longer continue to run. They would be upon him within minutes if he tried to flee into the scrub.

Dismounting stiffly, he slapped the horse's rump, sent it off into the brush and settled down in a narrow rift between two rising walls of rock. He moved quickly to the eastern end of it, keeping cover, until he could see the dusty stretch on the edge of the desert on his side of the river. The last of the outlaws kicked against his horse's flank, urging the animal out of the water. For a moment, the men stood in a tight bunch, talking among themselves, then he saw one point at the ground, knew that they had found his trail. Then started forward at once.

The sun was hot on his head and shoulders as he lay there against the burning rock. Fighting against sleep was a constant effort, even though he knew that to close his eyes for a single instant was to invite death. Eyes narrowed against the glare, acutely conscious of the throbbing pain in the side of his head, he tried to keep a close watch on the approaching men. He doubted if they would attack him in a bunch like that. To do so, would be to risk having every one of them shot down within seconds. A moment later, they began to run out, two of the men urging their mounts to the left, obviously intending to cut into the brush and try to cut off any line of retreat there might be back through the hills.

He tightened his lips, pulled the Colts from their holsters and held them carefully balanced in his hands. There was no underestimating the odds against him. They were stacked far higher than he could ever remember them. Seven outlaws against one man, and that man was wounded and weakened by hunger and thirst and with the blazing disc of the sun glaring in his eyes.

Savagely, he jerked himself upright. Once, he heard the snicker of one of the horses, paused tightly, expecting an answering call from his, but it never came. Relaxing, he lay back against the smooth rock. Seven desperate men, he thought bitterly. The heaviness of defeat lay deeply within him.

Down below him, where the brush thinned and dwarfed off into scrub, he waited until the four men, coming straight towards his hiding place, came within range of his guns. More than ever, he wished that he had thought to bring one of the high-powered rifles with him from the massacred wagon train. It would have stood him in good stead at that very moment, giving him a marked advantage over these men.

His eyes now were for the leading man, reading wicked purpose in the way he sat the saddle, a purpose which took shape in the slash of spurs along the flanks of the cayuse. The cruel goading sent the horse rearing forward along the narrow track between the rearing boulders of rock, outpacing the other men behind him. Savagely, Steve snapped a couple of shots at the other, saw the man sway in the saddle,

49

jerking hard on the reins to pull the horse's head round. The bewildered animal reared high on hind legs, threatening to unseat its rider. Steve's third bullet ricocheted off the rock, went whining into the distance, stopping the three other riders in their tracks. Hastily, they withdrew, out of sight among the boulders.

Steve lowered his guns and waited. Now they knew exactly where he was hiding out. It would not be long before they decided on a plan of action. Either they would try to rush him from several different directions, or they would try to sit him out, knowing that he would have to make a move soon, relying on the terrible heat of the sun to do the dirty work for them.

A moment later, a hoarse voice from among the boulders yelled: 'We know you're in there. Better come on out with yore hands high, or we'll have to come in and git you.'

Steve smiled thinly. 'Show yore faces and I'll put a bullet through yore heads,' he called back.

An uneasy pause, then: 'Listen, mister, whoever you are. We don't mean no harm. But you opened fire on us without warning. Just what are you trying to do?'

50

Steve threw a quick glance to his right, in the direction where the other two men had disappeared. He knew their game now. These men in front of him were trying to keep his attention focused on them while the other outlaws worked their way around on his flank and took him from the right. By now, they would have heard the shooting and know what it meant.

Presently, he saw the rustle in the bushes a hundred yards to his right, where the rock wall rose steeply for perhaps thirty or forty feet. From there, the outlaws could look down and pick him off quite easily. There was no cover for him in that direction. It was doubtful if a sixgun bullet would reach that far with any degree of accuracy, nevertheless, as the bushes parted and he caught a glimpse of the outlaw's face, he snapped two quick shots towards the rock face. The man threw himself backward with a sudden, savage yell as both bullets struck home. A moment later, the bushes parted again and the man's body toppled forward, over the lip of the rock, plunging down into the rocks below where it hit limply, then rolled out of sight.

As if it had been a signal, a volley of shots crashed from the position in front of him.

Bullets zipped and whined among the rocks close to his head as he pulled himself back, out of sight, unhurriedly reloading the Colt from his belt. Pretty soon, he decided, they would rush him. Now that their flank attack had failed and they knew he was on the alert for another sneak assault like that, they would come at him in a loose bunch. He pulled his lips back over his teeth as he waited for them to show themselves. For several minutes there was no sound but the occasional scrape of a hoof on rock. He wiped the sweat off his forehead with the sleeve of his shirt, screwing up his eyes against the sun.

Gripping his guns hard, he fired instinctively as more shots came from the scrub. Slitting his eyes against the muzzle flashes, he thumbed the hammer of his Colts swiftly so that the shots seemed to blur into a single sound. He saw one man fall on to the trail, but the answering blast of fire was immediate and accurate. He sucked in a deep breath and steadied himself. This was what the others wanted him to do, use up all of his ammunition, then step in and take him. A bullet struck the rock just above his head, raining down flakes of dirt on to his face. His skin was beginning to crawl and he felt the sweat gathering in little pools on his body, but now he was suddenly done with fear, finished with the waiting. This was part of the vengeance he had promised himself.

Overhead, the sun passed its zenith, but the terrible heat increased. There was a dull sickness in the pit of his stomach and his vision kept blurring now so that it was almost impossible to make out details around him. The sunglow which filled the hills and the overhead dust was sickening and the heat waves which bounded off the rock, refracted from the hills all around him, beat in endless waves against his face, forcing their way into his brain, even through lowered lids. A few buzzards were visible, wheeling like tattered strips of black cloth against the blue-white of the sky. He drank the last of the water in the canteen. There was barely sufficient to wet his lips and what there was was soon soaked up by the dry, swollen tongue, so that scarcely any of it reached his throat. There was no shade here, no place to escape the terrible, fiery, pitiless glare of the sun. He sat silent, speculating. As yet, he had no plan to put into action, in an attempt to get out of this place. The outlaws were still there, along the trail a piece, as yet making no attempt to attack him, content to wait things out and leave the first move to him.

The silence continued, grew long, filled with tension and he propped himself up cautiously on one elbow, lifted his head an inch at a time, peering through the bushes in the direction of the outlaw position. He could see nothing. They were content to keep under cover, knowing that he had little ammunition left and was not likely to shoot at shadows.

His head began to droop forward and he jerked his head savagely upright, cursing the moment of drowsiness, knowing that it might well have been his last, that the renegades were just waiting for him to go to sleep, to surrender his weary, pain-filled body to the fatigue which was dragging at each individual muscle. A single shot rang out. The Colts leapt into his hands as he pushed himself a little further down the rocky slope, until his heels touched the bottom. He half-expected to hear the whining shriek of a ricochet, speeding away from him into the brush, but the sound which followed that shot was one he had not expected, had not foreseen. There came the harsh, whinnying neigh of his horse and throwing back his head he saw it for a brief moment as it came out into the open. The bullet must have scorched along its hide, for it turned and galloped headlong into the brush and as he lay there, sucking air into his lungs, he heard the sound of hoofs fading swiftly into the distance. It would not come back, he thought defeatedly. Now they had him trapped like an animal with no hope of escape. He had made his way across that terrible, burning hell of a desert, only to perish here, at a point where he ought to have been safe.

How long could he last here, in this bone-drying heat? A half hour...? An hour possibly...? He pushed himself away from the hot rock as another volley of gunfire crashed out in the narrow valley. A dark figure threw itself forward, across the track a short distance away, a man who ran with his head well down to present a difficult target. But quick as the other was, possibly hoping to make his move by surprise, Steve's bullet caught him in the shoulder and he fell awkwardly as he tried to get under cover.

The gunfire died away. Evidently it had been intended only to force him to keep his head down while the gunslinger had made his attempt to get across to the other side of the trail. A moment later, that same harsh voice called out to him: 'Why don't you see sense, Mister? You can't get away from there and yore hoss is miles away by now and it won't come back. You're finished. May as well give yourself up – throw out yore gun and step this way with yore hands lifted.'

Steve answered the voice with a shot, aiming it carefully at the point from where he guessed the voice had come. Silence came close on the heels of the quivering echoes which chased themselves around the rearing columns of rock.

This was going to be a grim business. Grim and cold. With no quarter given to the vanquished. No mercy. These men wanted him dead. If he escaped, then others would know, the wagon trains that came across the alkali wastes would bring armed men with them, expecting trouble, and the outlaws would get nothing from their raids.

Still they waited, determined to sit it out. Sweat poured from his body as he leaned against the rock, and his arms and legs felt swollen. The long night without sleep began to tell on him. More than once, his eyes lidded and jerked and he pulled himself alert only just in time as something moved down the slope. Gradually, the sun began to lower itself towards the west. Shadows lengthened and some of the heat dissipated. Slowly, he worked his way along the narrow valley, reached the other end and checked the terrain in front of him. Silence lay over everything, a tight uneasy silence like the lull which preceded the storm. A rifle barked and he flinched as the bullet hummed close, striking the rock nearby. So they were still there, still alert, possibly taking it in turn to keep a close watch on him, waiting for him to sleep or go mad with the terrible heat.

When they finally made to rush him, he was almost caught off guard. They had circled slightly so as to come at him from the south and bullets were humming all about him before he finally woke to his danger and brought his own guns to bear. He squeezed the triggers savagely, felt the heavy Colts kick and buck against his wrists, saw one man go down, flopping forward on to his face, saw the others throw themselves down hard, squirming behind outcropping rocks and boulders for cover. But they had got within twenty yards of him now. The next time they came, he would not be able to stop all of them. And he knew with a sick certainty that this was merely a small portion of the whole outlaw band that had attacked the wagon train out there in the desert. There had been no sign of the man who had led that earlier raid, the man Steve had sworn would one day stand before his guns and know his vengeance.

These men had been considered more than enough to take care of him, to ride him down and destroy him before he could become a real menace to them. Rolling over on one side, he checked the bullets left in the guns and in the pouches of his belt. Twelve more left and the outlaws would make certain that few of them found their mark. He dashed the sweat from his brows, where it began to run into his eyes, half blinding him. Ground-tying, he edged back under cover, glancing behind him in the direction of the trees which grew on top of the slope. Once in there, among them he might stand a chance. But there was a lot of open ground to cross before he reached them, ground where he would make a perfect target for those men down there who were thirsting for his blood. His keen gaze took in every fold in the ground, knowing that here it could mean the difference between life and death for him. Very carefully, he edged his way back, keeping the rocky rise between the outlaws and himself. It was just possible, he told himself fiercely, that he might find his horse up there, somewhere still among the trees, and once mounted, he stood a chance of shaking off the men still alive.

He sank low and took his time, pausing only to throw quick glances over his shoulder as he made his way back towards the steep slope. There were long shadows here in which he could crouch and conceal himself, but as he broke cover and ran, hunched over, across the open ground, shots rattled after him as he had expected. He sprayed his right Colt empty among the men below as they moved after him with loud yells, certainly wounding one of them. But the others came on. His own shots had caused a little confusion among them and this, more than anything else, made them shoot wildly.

Having done what he wanted to do – to deter them for a little while – he ran diagonally across a pair of smooth, treacherous boulders, leaping from one to the other, throwing himself down out of sight behind the last, breathing heavily, his lungs hurting inside his chest from the exertion. His condition was growing steadily worse and the wound on the side of his head had opened and blood was dripping down the side of his face. He could not go on like this much longer, he knew, but to pause meant death. Now, he was halfway up the slope, but the trees which offered him conceal-ment were as far off as ever. The outlaws had fanned out now, still on foot, and were closing in on him from three sides. He could not move without exposing himself.

He loaded the remaining shells into the guns and waited. At least, he thought grimly, he could take a few of this hellion crew with him before he died. Two of them edged out into the open, urged forward by the tall man who led them. They ran for half a dozen paces, then went down again, out of sight. They were trying deliberately to draw his fire, to force him to expend his remaining bullets, leaving him helpless. He snapped two quick shots at the men, both missed.

Five minutes later, sensing that he was almost finished, they moved in purposefully for the kill. Five shots – no more. The hammers clicked on empty cartridge cases in the guns. The outlaws were still cautious as he ceased firing. At the moment, they were unsure as to whether or not he was completely out of ammunition; in a few seconds, they would be sure and–

They came out boldly into the open and began to walk forward, their guns in their hands, ready to shoot the minute they saw him clearly, but in that same instant, without warning of any kind, a rifle barked viciously from the trees at the head of the slope. One of the men dropped to his knees, guns falling from nerveless fingers. Another shot and a second man fell sideways, slumped over one of the boulders. The rest paused for a moment, stared up beyond the spot where Steve lay, then turned and fled back along the way they had come. Two more rifle shots sped after them as Steve pushed himself very slowly to his feet and stared after them. He was still standing there and staring down the slope when he heard the sound of their horses being put to a fast gallop, spotted them a little while later, mere dots as they cut out into the desert and headed for the river.

Steve shook his head a little to clear it. There was movement in the brush some fifty yards away and someone stepped out into the open, holding a rifle. Steve stared, scarcely able to believe his eyes as the woman came forward. A tall, red-haired woman with clear white skin and eyes that stared at him with the colour of ancient jade. With an effort, he pulled himself upright and hobbled towards her, pulling himself over the ground, every step sending a stab of agony through his body. The green eyes wandered over Steve, appraising him, then narrowed a little as they saw the blood on the side of his head. The trace of a smile grew on her lips.

'It seems we arrived just in time. Those coyotes won't stop until they hit the desert.' She reached out as he swayed on his feet, fought for the strength to stand. Behind her, he saw another figure step out of the trees and come down the slope towards them. All of the weariness of the past three days seemed to pour over him in an overwhelming flood so that he could scarcely stand. His head rolled forward and his knees sagged....

With an effort, Steve Yarborough lifted his head and looked about him. Several seconds passed before any recognition came. The room in which he found himself looked strange, plainly furnished, with curtains over the wide windows. He pushed himself up on to his elbows. The pain in his head had subsided to a dull ache and as he put up his right hand to touch it, he found that a bandage had been wound around it. A moment later, the door of the small room opened and the man he had seen on the trail shortly before he had blacked out, came in.

'Feeling better now, cowboy?' he asked, seating himself in the chair just inside the door. 'That was a pretty bad head wound you had there, looked as if it had been creased by a bullet.'

Steve nodded slowly. 'It had,' he agreed. 'Ran into some gun trouble out there in the desert, about three days before you found me.'

The other nodded. 'Guessed you might be from that wagon train,' he said nonchalantly. 'By the way, my name's Tennant. Clancy Tennant. I own this ranch and spread. My daughter Sarah is fixing you some food. Reckon you could do with it after what you've been through.'

'How long have I been unconscious?' asked Steve. His legs still felt weak and he did not trust himself to get out of bed and stand up.

'Close on two days. We fixed up that wound in your head. Your sorrel is stabled too. You must have ridden him hard to get away from those coyotes.'

'I did. Thought I wouldn't make it until you showed up. Reckon you saved my life. How come you managed to find me out there?'

'Your horse showed up here with a bullet wound in the flank. I guessed that something was wrong and we headed that way after we heard rifle fire. They must have wanted to kill you pretty badly to have hunted you all that way. Those outlaws don't usually come as far west as this unless they have to.'

'So you know them too,' mused Steve quietly. He lay back on the bed and stared up at the ceiling over his head for a long moment. He seemed to be safe at the moment, but as soon as he was fit again, he had work to do. From the other man's words, it was obvious that he was somewhere on the edge of the cattle country which lay at the foot of the mountains, between them and the desert. There was a small township somewhere in the area and as soon as he was well, he would ride over there and have a word with the sheriff. It was possible that they could get word through to Freeman City about what had happened. The sooner other wagon trains heading in that direction knew what to expect and took the proper precautions, the better.

'We've suffered at the hands of these renegades,' confirmed the other thickly. There was a tight expression on his face and a bleak look in his eyes. 'Nobody knows who leads them, but we do know that they're working hand in hand with Gruber. So far, we've never been able to get any evidence of that.'

'Gruber?' Steve stared across at Tennant. 'Seems to me I've heard that name before.'

'Could be if you've ever been in these parts before. Bart Gruber. He's one of the biggest and most powerful ranch owners in the whole of the territory. Owns most of the cattle around here, although how he got it is another matter.'

'You figure that he's rustled it?' Steve's brows went up a fraction of an inch. 'Or is there something more to it than that?'

'A lot more.' The other's face was hard. 'He's bought out a lot of the smaller ranchers in these parts. Those who wouldn't sell either met with an accident or had their cattle stolen by these outlaws. When they couldn't make their payments on the mortgages, all of which are held by the bank in Twin Buttes, Gruber's bank, he foreclosed on them and took over their ranches.'

'Can't you stop him? Surely there must be some law and order in Twin Buttes.'

'Gruber is the law. With these renegades at the back of him, nobody dares to rise against him. He has close on forty hands on his ranch and God alone knows how many gunslingers there are out there in the desert, preying on the wagon trains heading west. When we found you, it wasn't difficult to guess what had happened. They don't usually leave any survivors – too risky.'

Steve nodded grimly, tightening his lips. The grey eyes snapped as he looked across at the rancher. 'They didn't intend that I should get away,' he said slowly. 'If it hadn't been for your timely intervention, I would have been buzzard meat by now.'

The other rose heavily to his feet. 'Best get some rest,' he said quietly, softly. There came a knock at the door and he opened it, to admit Sarah Tennant, carrying a tray in her hands. She set it down on the small table beside the bed and flashed him a broad smile.

'I made all of this myself,' she said, 'so you will have to eat it all. You don't seem to have had anything to eat for several days.'

He sipped the cup of black coffee, felt the warmth come back into his stomach and then ate silently of the plate which she placed before him. There were sweet potatoes, sowbelly and beans and for the first time, he realized just how hungry he really was. Not until he had finished and had pushed the empty plate away, leaning back on the pillow, did Clancy Tennant speak.

'How many were there in that wagon train, son?' he asked tightly.

Steve pursed his lips. 'I don't rightly know,' he said, slowly. 'Close on three dozen. They never stood a chance, hit us before we knew they were there. I'd spotted the remains of their camp fire, but Madison, he was the wagon master, figured that they wouldn't attack us before we had some warning of their presence. He reckoned that they would come from up ahead, but they had circled and took us from the rear. We killed about seven of them but there were more than a score of men in that band. We couldn't kill them all. They fired the wagons and then slaughtered everyone there, men, women and children. They left nothing. I was knocked cold when that bullet creased my skull, otherwise I would have been killed too. They must have discovered I was still alive when they went back. They trailed me across the river and surrounded me in the foothills. That was when you showed up, just as I'd fired my last bullet.'

'Glad to have been of help.' The other leaned back in his chair and ran a finger down the side of his nose. 'I suppose you'll be riding on west once you're fit to travel again. Heading out for California, I'll be bound.'

'I was.' Steve admitted. 'But I changed my mind when that wagon train was destroyed. I swore then that I'd kill those men and in particular the man who led them and I aim to do just that before I leave this territory.'

The news seemed to please the rancher, for he nodded his head several times as if satisfied. Slowly, he got to his feet, stood looking down at Steve for a long moment, then said: 'We'll have a long talk together, you and I, when you feel stronger. I have an idea that we may be able to help each other.'

He went out of the room, closing the door behind him. Sarah Tennant came in a moment later, for the tray. 'We'll soon have you on your feet again,' she said brightly. 'Once you've been fed and rested.'

He eyed her speculatively for a moment. 'This outlaw band,' he began softly: 'if they know that you helped me, and they come here for me, what will they do to you and your father?'

'They won't find you,' she said confidently. She walked over and examined the bandage around his head.

'But if they do, they'll kill both of you; just as they murdered those men and women on the wagon train.'

'Perhaps.' She smiled and there was nothing of fear in the jade-green eyes which regarded him steadily. 'But that's a threat they've made against us for over a year now. It's only a matter of time before they try to carry it out.'

'And aren't you afraid?' he asked in surprise.

'A little. But we knew the risks we had to take and the dangers to be faced when we first came out here. This is wild country. It will be many years before it is tamed sufficiently for us to have proper law and order, and men like Gruber have been put where they belong. It's up to people like us to stop him from taking over the country. Perhaps that's why we stay.'

He lay back, thinking hard. It was all right

for him to face up to these outlaws – killing and destroying had been a part of his life for so long now, that he could scarcely remember a time when he had not been forced to live by the gun. But there was no reason why he should bring these two people into it, especially after they had saved his life.

'I know what you're thinking,' said the girl at length. 'But this is our fight now, as well as yours. If we're to survive here, we have to fight Gruber and his gunslingers.' Her face was tight and the green eyes flashed in the sunlight which streamed through the half-open windows.

'You don't stand a chance against those men,' he retorted harshly. 'I've seen them. I know what they can do and how they work. They'll strike in the night and burn the ranch down about your ears, stampede your cattle, and shoot you down in cold blood, laughing while they do it. I saw them massacre the women and children on that wagon train.'

'We heard that it was leaving Freeman City over a week ago. But they said that it had an escort of troops for the desert crossing. Evidently, those were just rumours. The nearest troops are at Carson Wells and they wouldn't be spared just for a wagon train.

When it didn't pass through here on its way into Twin Buttes, we knew what had happened.'

'They had their spies everywhere, in Freeman City. They knew when we were due to move out, how much gold was being carried and how many rifles and Colts they would have ranged against them. They could pick their time and place and we never stood a chance.'

He fingered the bandage around his head absently for a moment, then allowed his hand to fall to his side. The wound would soon heal and then he would have to leave this ranch and head out for Twin Buttes. There, he might learn something, might be able to rouse the townsfolk against this man Gruber, who seemed to be at the back of all the trouble in this territory.

As the days passed, Steve Yarborough slowly regained his strength. The wound along the side of his scalp healed and although his right arm was stiff and sore where he had fallen some time in the past, he made it work. Each night and morning, for a solid hour, he exercised it, forced it to work. Unless he regained some of his old speed, he was as good as dead. Methodically, swiftly, his hand, the fingers outspread, dropped for

71

the gun in the holster at his waist, bringing it upwards, the hammer clicking on an empty chamber. The burning desire for revenge was still there, if anything growing stronger with every passing day. The picture in his mind of that man who had led the attack on the wagon train never faded. Sooner or later, he knew, he and that man would come face to face, and it would be an encounter from which only one of them would live to walk away.

The outlaws seemed to have made no attempt during the days he had been there to search the surrounding territory for him. He began to have the feeling that perhaps his earlier fears about them had been unfounded.

On the ninth day, he broached the subject of riding into Twin Buttes with Clancy Tennant. The older man listened to him patiently, then shook his head. 'I say you'd be a goddurned fool to show your face inside the town,' he declared emphatically. 'They'll have your face on every wanted poster in this country.'

Steve stared at him in surprise. 'Wanted posters,' he said dully.

'Sure. That's the way they work, hand in glove with Gruber. There ain't no law in

Twin Buttes right now. Last sheriff tried to go out after that gang and was brought back over the saddle of his horse. Since then, nobody has upped and taken the job. That leaves Gruber in sole command there.'

3

THE WILD BREED

The next day, Steve rose to find the sunlight shining straight into the small room to the rear of the ranchhouse. He tried to sit up in the bed, and found that now he was able to do so without the room spinning dizzyingly around him and his legs no longer felt so weak at the knees when he swung them to the floor and stood up. He went over to the window, rubbing the back of his hand over the bristles on his chin. Slowly and carefully, he felt for the bandage on his head. It was still there, but he knew that underneath it, the flesh was healing quickly and that soon, he would be able to move out of this place, remove the danger which his presence there meant to these two people, and ride into Twin Buttes, where he figured he might find the answers to a lot of the questions that had been bothering him since the wagon train had been jumped by that outlaw band. There was a jugful of cold water and a basin on the dresser and he washed his face with it, feeling it shock some of the taut awareness back into his body, flooding away the weariness which had lain deep within him for the past few days. He flexed his fingers, stared down at them for a long moment, then nodded to himself, satisfied.

When the time came for him to use his guns again, he would be ready. Back in Dodge and around Abilene, he had been known as one of the fastest gunmen in the territory. A man who walked neither with the law nor the killers who crowded the state; a lone wolf, who preferred to right any wrongs which came his way by his own code of vengeance.

The door opened ten minutes later, after he had shaved with the razor he found beside the water basin. Sarah Tennant came in. She was wearing a white silk shirt, open at the neck, and riding boots similar to those she had worn when he had first met her. He noticed the worried look at the back of the green eyes instantly, even though she smiled broadly at him.

'How are you feeling this morning, Steve?' she asked gently.

He grinned. 'A lot better than yesterday,' he said quietly. 'But you look troubled. Has anything happened while I've been asleep?'

'We're not sure.' She frowned. Her eyes were faintly puzzled as she looked steadily at him, as if she saw something in him that she hadn't expected to find. She went over to the window and stared out for a long moment before speaking. Then she turned and faced him. 'One of the ranches fifteen miles away was attacked and burnt last night. We heard ten minutes ago from one of the men who worked there. Jess Ordway and his wife were killed in the firing. Their baby daughter was found in the barn where someone had taken her for safety. She's being cared for in town.'

Steve sucked in a deep, sharp breath. For a moment, the tightness came back into his mind and his fingers clenched by his sides. But his voice was calm and oddly unhurried as he said: 'You think it was that same bunch of outlaws that attacked the wagon train? Is that what's on your mind?'

'We think so. Either that, or it was some of Gruber's men. Makes no difference really, they both work for him, carry out his orders. The Ordways were asked to sell their ranch to Gruber ten days ago. They refused like most of the others. Jess reckoned that he could count on his hands to help him if there was any gunplay. Seems he was wrong about that. They all left as soon as these renegades attacked the place. Left him and his wife to die.'

'And you say there's no sheriff in Twin Buttes?'

'Gruber has been campaigning to put one of his own men into that position, but most of the townsfolk are against it. They know what it will mean and at the moment he isn't quite strong enough to go against the whole town. But if they don't elect a sheriff soon, then he'll he able to fill that post with whoever he likes, by law. And there'll be nothing anyone can do to stop him.'

Steve's fingers tightened convulsively. Then he forced himself to relax. This was really no concern of his. All he wanted was to find that man who had led those outlaws and kill him. After that, he wanted to get astride his horse and head out for California. He wanted no part of a place such as Twin Buttes.

'Surely if the ranchers united, they ought to be able to run this crook out of the territory, and his outlaw friends. But if they go on as they are right now, he'll take them all, one at a time, and by the time they wake up to the danger it will be too late.'

Sarah Tennant forced a weary smile. 'They're afraid, all of them. They need someone strong who can lead them against Gruber and his killers. Without that, they are helpless, like sheep.'

'But why tell me this?' He raised the dark brows a little and regarded her curiously.

'Don't you think that you might be able to help them?' she said quietly.

'No.' He shook his head, buckled the heavy belt around his middle.

'Why not?' There was a sudden sharpness in her voice which he had not heard before. He lifted his head and looked at her in the sunlight. She went on quickly: 'I know that it might not be right to bother you with our troubles. We got ourselves into this mess and it's up to us to find a way out of it. But perhaps you might like to know how it started. Gruber is a gambler, Steve. One of the worst kind because he gambles, not for money, but for power and he deals in human beings instead of dollar bills. He started to buy up land shortly after he rode into Twin Buttes from some place back east. Nobody knew much about him in those days, except that he used to play cards with almost everybody and when they lost to him and couldn't pay, he just smiled and said he'd take a note on their land and ranches just to make the notes legal. Everyone figured him for a good man who'd let them have the notes back once they won. But they never seemed to have a winning streak once they'd signed over their ranches. Then came a time when Gruber wasn't smiling any more. He suddenly demanded the money or the land and most of them had to get out and leave. To add insult to injury, he kept a few of them on as hired hands.'

Steve nodded, and let her continue talking. He knew how this had come about. There would be no thought in these people's minds that perhaps Gruber was working with a marked deck or using a gang of professional cardsharps in his business. Like all gamblers, they went on the assumption that the next card to be turned over would be their lucky card, that they would be able to recoup all of their losses on a single winning streak. But by that time, they were in this dirty game up to their necks and there was no easy way out for them. No doubt Gruber had been devilishly clever, but such men always were.

'Then,' went on the girl slowly, 'Twin Buttes woke up one day and found that Gruber was no longer the man who had ridden into town with little more than a horse and a handful of dollars. He had grown a lot bigger in those few months and everyone was wondering how it had happened without them noticing it. They found that he had been buying up a lot of land quietly, using agents that he had brought in from back east to help him in this deal. And worse still, he had hired a gang of gunmen to help him collect on any outstanding debts, just in case anyone turned nasty and decided not to pay up. That was how he managed to take over most of the land around here, and all of it rich cattle country. His herd soon totalled close on thirty thousand head and it's still growing. Very few of them were come by honestly.'

'I see.' Steve checked the guns hanging low at his waist. He nodded his head slowly. 'And no one tried to make a stand against him?'

'Some did. One of the biggest ranchers gathered some of his men together and rode into Twin Buttes looking for him. But Gruber had been warned that he was on his way and was waiting for him in town. There was a gunfight and the rancher was killed and most of his men shot from ambush. They never had a chance. Very few tried to go against him after that.'

Steve rubbed his chin thoughtfully. 'And what makes you think that I could help you in this?' He eyed her closely. 'One man can't do anything against a band like that. I know – I saw what they did to that wagon train.' There was no sign that he was recalling that night when he had seen his companions killed in cold blood; no sign unless it could be read in the hand hovered a little way over the butt of the heavy Colt, fingers tensed.

For a time, there was silence in the room, then he shifted his feet uneasily and said quietly: 'I swore out there in the desert that I would kill the man who led those outlaws. I also owe you my life and–'

'We only did what any other decent people would have done in the circumstances.' she said quietly, not looking at him, 'You owe us nothing.'

'Perhaps. But that isn't the way I look at it. I reckon I'll ride into Twin Buttes and take a look round for myself. If there is a tie-in between Gruber and those outlaws, perhaps we have a common cause, you and I.'

She smiled now, suddenly unafraid. 'It may be,' said Sarah quietly. 'I hope so. If this country is to grow up and take its proper place, it will have to get rid of all lawless elements. There's no place here for the wild breed.' Her voice was low and husky. She eyed him closely for a few minutes longer, then turned towards the door. 'I'll fix you something to eat, Steve, if you're to ride into Twin Buttes, you'll need something nourishing inside you.' At the door she paused, turning: 'And be careful of Gruber. That rancher who went in to face him – Gruber killed him in a fair fight. Don't let him fool you, Steve. He's one of the fastest gunmen in the territory, but he always sees to it that the odds are stacked against the man he intends to kill. He never takes chances.'

'I'll be careful,' he said with an ominous quietness. 'And thanks for the warning.'

She went out of the room, closing the door softly behind her and he stood for a long moment by the window, turning things over in his mind. It seemed he had let himself in for a lot more than he had bargained for when he had been brought here by this red-haired girl and her father. She was a fighter, he thought admiringly, a woman who knew fear but who could keep it under tight control. Her father too, had struck him as a man who did not give up easily. If it came to a showdown with this man Gruber, they would fight to defend their home. He thought again of the ranch which had been burned to the ground during the night, and a little shiver of anger went through him. This was the usual pattern of events, one he had seen practised and repeated over the whole of the west. A man set himself up in a position of power and began to eliminate any opposition, gradually bringing in hired killers to do the dirty work for him, doing his best to cover up his plans so that they might appear legal. It was not entirely unknown for the Rangers to take a hand in these matters if they assumed important proportions and for that reason these crooks normally had lawyers as crooked as themselves to make everything appear legal, often went to the extreme of having the sheriffs in their pay. Anyone who attempted to stop them usually met with a quick end, or perhaps a planned murder might put an end to these activities.

He went into the small parlour five minutes later. There was the smell of bacon coming from the kitchen and Clancy Tennant came in a moment later. He gave Steve a quick grin. 'I gather that Sarah had been talking to you about our troubles, Steve,' he said genially. 'I hope you won't be feeling obligated to us in any way. We know that we have no right to ask you to remain here and help us in this matter. It may be that nobody can help us now. Gruber's too big and influential. His word is law in this territory.'

Sarah brought in the breakfast and Steve ate ravenously, washing down the food with the excellent coffee. Even as he ate, his mind was busy, thinking over what he had been told about this man Gruber, the way he went about making himself the biggest and most powerful man in the territory. Finally, the meal over, he rose to his feet. 'I reckon I'll ride into town by way of that ranch that was attacked during the night,' he said, forcing casualness into his voice. 'Perhaps you could tell me which way to go.'

Sarah Tennant looked at him curiously for a moment, eyes narrowed a little, then said: 'I'll ride with you, Steve.' She was facing him now. The light and humour had fled from her eyes and they were hard like jade. Steve sensed the change in her, hesitated for a moment, then threw a quick glance towards her father. The other nodded slowly: 'You may as well let her ride with you Steve,' said the other softly. 'She's stubborn and determined. Once she's set her mind on something nothing will change it. Takes after her mother in that respect, I reckon.'

Steve hesitated for a second longer, then nodded. 'Very well, I'll be glad if you'll show me the way, Sarah.' As they moved out of the ranch and into the small courtyard, he was conscious more than ever of the closeness of her and of the strong attraction that he seemed to feel for this red-haired, courageous girl. It must have been hard living out here during the years they had been there, he reflected, as he swung himself up into the saddle and sat easily, waiting for her. He moved his shoulders to ease them in the half round of the saddle, staring ahead of him for a moment to where the trail wound between tall trees that stood atop a low rise. Beyond the trees, he knew, lay cattle country, flat land with lush, green grass, where they could breed some of the best beef in the whole of the country. It was a beautiful place and he did not blame the girl and her father for wanting to fight to keep it, to hold it against men like Gruber. His teeth were tight shut and his lips were closed as he urged the sorrel forward, the girl beside him, riding easily. He noticed the rifle thrust into the scabbard beside the saddle. Evidently, she intended taking no chances.

The trail wound beneath the cool shade of

the trees and there was the sharp, sweet smell of pines in his nostrils. The sun had lifted a few degrees above the horizon and it was still cool there as they rode down the far side of the slope, into the stretching cattle country. There were close on a thousand head of cattle on the prairie, he noticed, all of them sleek, well-fed animals, with the Double S brand. A peaceful, calm country, where it seemed difficult to believe that it needed only one spark to ignite the whole powder-barrel of a range war. That was the last thing anyone here wanted, he reflected; but it would come if Gruber persisted in his efforts to take over control of the entire area.

He forced himself to speak, keeping calmness in his tone. 'These people who were attacked and killed during the night – were they friends of yours?'

She nodded. For an instant, he thought he detected the brightness of tears in her eyes, but she jerked her head a little and he could not be sure for when she looked in his direction again, they were perfectly dry. 'We came here with them in the same wagon train, almost fifteen years ago. They were looking for a place to settle down and raise children, a place where they could feel secure. They never thought that it would end like this.'

He nodded tightly and fell silent, not wanting to pursue this painful subject. Hell would break loose once it came to the inevitable showdown, but he didn't want to think of that just yet. There were too many other thoughts in his mind demanding his attention. An hour later, they rode along the bank of a wide river which divided one part of the prairie from another. The sun was lifting rapidly now, burning hot on his head and shoulders as he sat in the saddle. They followed the river for almost two miles, then forded it, setting their horses across at a spot where the river was shallow.

They did not talk now, as they cut across the range, heading towards the low hills in the sun-hazed distance. Out of the corner of his eye, Steve watched the girl curiously, closely. Several times, he saw her gaze turn to some point which must have held a meaning only for her. Then they rode over one of the rises and he found himself staring down into a wide, deep valley where a spring rose at the southern end, flowing north to join the river. The girl's gaze swung slowly, lingeringly, and he saw it rest on the blackened ruins down below them, ruins which still smouldered, hours after they had been set ablaze. He wondered if Sarah Tennant had been there when those walls had been built and the boards of the small bunkhouse had been set together. He glanced at her, saw the hard, stubborn set of her mouth and chin, the dry eyes, and the proud, almost defiant way she sat in the saddle, hands tight in front of her, resting on the pommel.

'I reckon I'll be riding down there to take a look around,' he said softly. 'If you want to stay here until I come back, it might be best.'

'No. I'll come down with you,' she said tautly. She put spurs to the horse and urged it down the slope. He followed quickly, aware of the uneasy silence which hung over everything in this valley now. Once, he thought tightly, it must have rung to the sounds of life and activity, to the words and laughter of a man and woman who built and planned for the future, only to have it snatched away from them because of the vicious greed of one man.

He reined the sorrel in front of the buildings, the acrid stench of smoke clinging to his nostrils. Destruction had been virtually complete. Whoever had destroyed this place had made an excellent job of it. Dismounting, he moved into the ruins. Splintered wood, which had not been burned in the fire, crunched noisily underfoot. There was a small cot in one corner of the lower room, lying on its side, the linen coverings little more than blackened, tattered strips of burnt cloth. He felt the coldness on his face moving down into the rest of his body as he stood there and looked about him at the remains of what had once been a proud and happy place. He wondered tightly if Gruber was proud of himself for having done this thing.

He hunted around for several minutes, without finding anything, then went back to where the girl still sat, stony-faced and hard-eyed. The knuckles of her hands stood out white under the skin as she held the reins tightly. She said thinly: 'They probably tried to blame it on Indians. But there are none in this part of the country.'

'This was the work of white men,' said Steve, confidently. 'I've seen enough of the handiwork of those outlaws to recognize it instantly. Let's get away from this place.' He climbed back into the saddle, turned the horse's head away from the ruined ranch and put it into a trot. There was a deep and rising anger within him, coming to the surface. He had always been a man slow to anger and there had been a time when the wildness rode him instead of being ridden, a hard and angry violence which over-rode everything else. They rode to the edge of the spread, were on the point of crossing the boundary fence, when there came the sound of horses on their right. A moment later, three men rode up to them, men bunched tightly together, their faces hard in the sunlight, under a thin filming of sweat and trail dust.

The leader, a short, wiry man with the narrow eyes of a cold-blooded killer edged his horse forward a little way, reining it swiftly. His eyes flicked from Steve to the girl, then back again, taking in the heavy Colts in their holsters. He gestured to the east, in the direction from which they had just ridden.

'You must be a stranger in these parts, mister,' said the other and his voice was almost a snarl. 'This is private rangeland. We don't like trespassers around these parts.'

Steve looked at him in mild surprise, feeling the tightness growing swiftly inside him. There was no mistaking the meaning behind the other's words. His eyes took in the men seated on their mounts behind him, their hands never very far from their guns.

'Reckon I must have got things wrong,' he said casually. 'I heard this ranch belonged to a young couple who built that ranch back there, that one which has been burned to the ground quite recently.'

The other's thin lips parted in a faint smile, but there was death in his eyes. 'You heard wrong, mister,' he said deliberately. 'This spread belongs to Bart Gruber and he don't like strangers riding over his grassland.'

'That's a downright lie.' Sarah Tennant sat tall and straight in her saddle, eyes glinting dangerously. 'If this land belongs to Gruber, then he stole it like the rest of the spreads he's taken over. He was behind the murder of those two people last night. Seems to me that's all the evidence we need.'

The smile turned into a snarl. The two men behind the other backed their mounts off a little way, expecting trouble, ready for it, knowing they had only a man and a girl to deal with.

'That's dangerous talk,' the sibilant voice held the same quality that Steve would have expected from a striking snake. 'We got orders to shoot to kill if anyone tries to pass

92

over this spread. Seems you've just talked yourselves into big trouble.' His hands moved from the pommel of the saddle, hovering close to his guns.

Steve read the danger in the other's eyes, saw the deadly purpose there and knew that he would have to kill all three men. 'Don't try to go for your guns, any of you,' he said thinly. His words were hard, positive things. Not argumentative. 'I can kill all three of you quite easily. I don't want to, but if you belong to Gruber's band of killers, then I reckon I'll make this place a lot cleaner if I do kill you.'

The other's eyes narrowed to mere slits. For a moment, it seemed there was hesitation in him at the quiet, calm words. Then he shrugged his shoulders quickly. His hands hovered over the guns, starting downward.

'Don't try it!'

All three men went for their guns in the same instant. They were fast draws, good draws, but Steve's hands had struck downward with the speed of a striking rattler. There were three shots, no more and smoke curled from the barrels of the heavy Colts. The two men to the rear slipped from their saddles and crashed to the ground, looks of astonishment frozen on to their faces, their guns dropping from their nerveless fingers as they fell.

The man who faced Steve remained upright in the saddle for a long moment, fighting to hold life in the eyes now wide and filled with a fear beyond life, looking in bewilderment at the man who had out-drawn and outshot him. The eyes continued to stare as he slipped forward over the pommel, resting there for an instant as if asleep, before he fell to the ground, his horse bucking and rearing a little, threaten-ing to trample the inert body under its hoofs.

'I hope that all three of them were among the men who attacked that ranch last night,' was all that Steve said, as he holstered the guns and turned to face the girl. There was a strange expression on her face, one which he had never seen before. Some inner flame at work, at the back of her eyes, just begin-ning to show through.

Skirting the stream which ran northward to feed the river, they came back on to the trail and headed into Twin Buttes. The town slumbered in the heat of the noonday sun. Dust lay in the streets and the main street seemed to shimmer and waver in front of them. They rode their horses slowly, feeling the eyes of the men on the boardwalks on them, watching, assessing every move they made. Curiosity tugged at Steve as he rode, giving no sign that he was aware of the close scrutiny. There seemed to be something ominous and threatening in the way the silence hung low over the town, seeming to hug the ground, like some thick and heavy blanket. They entered from the south end of the town and he kept his eyes alert for the sheriff's office, locating it finally where the main street branched into one of the narrower, side streets.

'You're not thinking of telling anyone about those three men you killed back there on the trail, are you?' asked Sarah in a tight, little voice, turning her head to look at him in sudden surprise. 'If you do, they'll kill you. Gruber won't allow you to live until sunset.'

He shook his head slowly. 'I reckon I know the temper of this town,' he said shortly. 'I could sense it the moment we rode in. These people are scared, afraid to make a single move for fear that they end up on a rope, with some trumped up charge levelled against them.' He felt the sun hot and red against his eyelids and his eyes stung. Dust from the trail had worked its way into the folds of his skin and he rubbed the back of his hand across his mouth. 'I figger I'll just report that we rode by the ranchhouse back there and discovered that it had been burned to the ground. I'd like to know what sort of story they intend to spread around.'

'Do you think that would be wise?' She deliberately kept her voice low, as if afraid that her words would be overheard by the men lounging in the shade of the store-fronts. 'If you tell them that, once they discover the bodies of those three men, they'll tie you in with their shooting.'

'Could be,' he admitted. 'But that's a risk I'll have to take. Besides, if they do decide to come gunning for me, I'll know where I stand.'

'They'll hang you from the nearest tree when they catch you,' she said drily, but there was a touch of admiration in her voice that was not lost on Steve.

He dismounted in front of the sheriff's office, tethered the sorrel to the hitching rail, and walked up on to the sidewalk. A man lounged in a wicker chair near the glass-panelled door, his feet on the wooden rail. He seemed to be asleep but as Steve came abreast of him, he raised one eyelid languorously and said with a slow drawl: 'If you're lookin' for the sheriff, we don't have one in this town.'

Steve paused, as if surprised, then rubbed his chin thoughtfully, 'If that's so,' he said quietly, 'who's the law in this town? You got a deputy around?'

'Guess you can call me that.' The other got slowly to his feet and eyed Steve closely, taking in everything with a careful, sweeping gaze. He had a thin, pinched face and shifty eyes; a dangerous man whose occupation, thought Steve wryly, would be shooting men in the back or from cover of ambush. Possibly one of the men who had shot down the riders with that rancher whom Gruber had killed.

He shrugged his shoulders nonchalantly. 'Reckon if you're the deputy, you're just the man I want to see.' He chose his words carefully, letting no expression flick over his features. 'Miss Tennant and I rode into town this morning. On the way we passed a ranch-house about five miles out of town. It had been burned down some time during the night, some of the wood still smouldering. Thought we'd better report it to the sheriff, in case he wanted to get a posse together and go after the critters who did it.'

The other raised his brows a fraction, took out his tobacco pouch and rolled himself a cigarette slowly. Running his tongue along the edge of the paper, he rolled it into a neat cylinder, evidently with long practice, then placed it between his lips and lit it, inhaling slowly, 'Reckon you must be a stranger around these parts, Mister,' he said finally. 'These things happen all the time in this territory. Especially since we lost the last sheriff. Nobody to go out after those pesky Indians now.'

So that was to be the story they intended to put around, thought Steve tightly. He doubted whether many of the ranchers and decent townsfolk would be fooled for a single instant; but so long as Gruber held the whip hand, they would say nothing against him. It wasn't worth it, especially when their own ranch might be the next to be fired.

Steve looked along the hot, dusty road, back in the direction from which he had ridden. Deliberately, he kept all trace of emotion out of his voice as he said quietly: 'Never figured you'd have trouble with Indians in this territory. Always thought they had pulled back to the west.'

'Sometimes,' said the other ominously, 'it isn't healthy to think too much.'

Steve felt the anger bubbling up inside him. He saw the other's gaze flick to the girl, where she sat high in the saddle, watching from the street. With an effort, he fought the savage anger down, swallowed it harshly. It came to him then that the other wanted him to draw, knowing that once he did, he placed himself on the wrong side of the law. Perhaps the other had already recognized him as a dangerous man who asked too many questions and seemed, on the face of things, to know too many answers.

'I'll remember that,' he said softly, then turned on his heel and walked back along the boardwalk, towards the horse. Every second, he was acutely aware of the other's eyes boring into his back. Reaching up for the reins, he was on the point of swinging himself up into the saddle, when a voice stopped him. It was a well-modulated, cultured voice, that came from the dimness of the boardwalk.

'You seem to be asking quite a lot of questions around here, stranger. Perhaps you'd like to put them to me. I may be able to answer some of them for you.'

He turned and stared at the frock-coated man, standing beside the deputy in front of the sheriff's office. The other was handsome in a smooth, suave way, and under the expensive exterior, he knew there was a body as hard as nails, tough and resilient.

'Perhaps,' he said hesitantly. 'But I'm afraid I don't.'

'We all know the kind of answers you give, Gruber.' Sarah's voice, hard and brittle, reached him from the street. He turned and saw that she was staring intently at the other, a look of pure hate in the jade-green eyes.

Steve glanced back. So this was Bart Gruber, the man who was behind the killings, the burnings, and also, if rumour was to be believed, the man who gave the orders to the outlaw band in the desert to the east.

'Miss Tennant.' The other's voice lost none of its smoothness, in spite of what the girl had said. 'I realize that you've been listening to a lot of the rumours that have been spread around town about me. But I'd like to remind you that there's nothing whatever to prove any of them. Besides, haven't I helped your father with that ranch he has? He owes me quite a tidy sum of money, as you know, and I haven't been pressing him for it.'

'That will come, in time,' she said tightly. She dismounted, sliding to the ground, walking over to stand by Steve. 'But if you have any answers to Steve's questions, I'd like to hear them too.'

'By all means.' The other nodded casually, and led the way along the street, pausing in front of the batwing doors of one of the saloons. He pushed them open and stepped inside. Steve followed close on his heels, eyes alert for any sign of trouble. There was always the possibility that this was a trap of some kind, and he had no intention of being shot in the back as was reputed to have happened to so many of Gruber's opponents.

The other said something in low tones to the man behind the bar, then led the way up the wide, curving stairway to the upper floor. At the end of a long corridor, he pushed open a door and stood on one side to allow them to enter.

'I've told Lou to send up a bottle of our very best brandy,' he said softly. 'I assure you that it is the finest in this part of the country.' He nodded towards one of the chairs, near the polished table, held one back for Sarah, then sat down himself, regarding them with a faint look of amusement on his somewhat arrogant features. He laced his fingers together on the table in front of him.

'Now, suppose you tell me what's been

troubling you,' he said quietly. 'I think that first of all, I should point out that I'm aware of the stories which have been going around about me, but I'm sure that a man like yourself will realize that every successful man has a lot of enemies. These people in Twin Buttes don't like the way I do my business, but if you want to get on in this world, you often have to be hard. I give the ranchers every possible chance to pay their debits. It isn't until they've shown quite clearly and convincingly that they aren't able to do so that I foreclose on their mortgages. But that's business. If I didn't do that I would soon be bankrupt myself.'

'And just how do they lose all this money to you, Mister Gruber?' asked Steve pointedly. 'I understood that they lost it at cards, here in your saloons. Funny that scarcely anyone ever seems to win.'

The other shrugged, gave no sign that he was aware of the tone of Steve's voice. 'I can't stop them from gambling if they want to, can I? After all, I'm here to provide entertainment for them. If they lose all of their money, that is nothing to do with me. They could always stop if things went against them.'

'Of course.' The touch of sarcasm in

Steve's voice was plain now. 'You know as well as I do that if a man has lost everything he has, he can't resist that one last stake on a card which might get it all back for him.'

The other opened his mouth to say something but at that moment there came a sharp knock on the door and a second later, it opened and the bartender came in with a tray bearing a tall, slender bottle and three glasses.

'I'm sure you're going to enjoy this,' said Gruber smoothly. He poured out the glasses, then lifted his and drank deeply. Steve sipped the brandy and in spite of his feelings towards the other was grudgingly forced to admit that it was excellent.

He sat back in his chair, eyeing the other closely. He wanted to see just where Gruber's curiosity would lead him. The other was still unsure about him, wanted to know why he was there and what he was doing in Twin Buttes, especially with Sarah Tennant. Gruber was a cautious man. He would not make a move until he was absolutely sure of himself. For all he knew, word of his activities here could have spread further than he had thought, and Steve might be a United States marshal, working undercover. If that were the case, it might not be wise to kill him openly. Besides, Gruber knew that there was still plenty of time in which to make any plans that were needed. It was unlikely that Steve would leave town and keep on riding.

'Now suppose we get down to business. You say that one of the ranches had been burnt to the ground, about five miles away and from what I heard, you don't think it was the work of Indians.' He drew the thick lips back into a tight smile. 'No need to deny it, I know what they say about me here. They say that I ordered my men to attack and burn that ranch, because the people there wouldn't pay what they owed to me, couldn't pay it, so I moved in on them without warning and made certain that I got it over their dead bodies. Now you'll have to admit that when people talk like that without any proof at all, a man has a right to defend himself. So I own most of the land in these parts and most of the cattle. But that isn't a crime, even here on the frontier.'

Steve leaned forward. 'They also say that you're in cahoots with those outlaws in the desert. Now they're something I do know about.'

He saw the sudden glint in the other's eyes

instantly. Then the guarded look came back, but Gruber hadn't been quick enough to hide it.

'That's a dirty lie,' he said harshly, savagely. 'I never worked with outlaws. Sure I know that there is a band operating out there, attacking the wagon trains as they move through. But I've nothing to do with them. Everything I have, I got legally. I can prove that.'

Steve drained his glass, gave a quick nod. 'If you say so, Gruber,' he said hoarsely, 'but I hope for your sake that what you say is true.' His voice took on a tight edge. 'You see, I was on that last wagon train they attacked. They set it ablaze and killed everyone on it – or so they thought. But a bullet creased my forehead, knocking me cold and they left me for dead. When they came back and discovered I had gone, they headed after me, hoping to run me down before I reached the edge of the desert. They almost succeeded in killing me. If it hadn't been for Miss Tennant and her father, they would have done. As it is, I'm still alive and I intend to kill every man in that band. And every man with anything to do with it. Seems there's no real law and order in this town, so I'll have to do it myself.'

Gruber's face was hard as he stared across at him, the blue eyes snapping angrily, his fingers bar-straight on the table in front of him.

4

SHERIFF OF LAWLESS

Steve reined his mount and looked across at Sarah Tennant quietly. There was an unspoken question in her glance and he knew, instinctively, what thoughts were passing through her mind at that moment. She said softly: 'Will you be riding back with me to the ranch, Steve? I won't make any pretence about it. We need you there, especially if Gruber does send his men out there to take the place from us by force.'

He bit his lower lip, then shook his head slowly. 'I figure I can do a lot more good here, Sarah. Besides, here I can learn of what Gruber does intend to do and I can reach the ranch long before his hired killers if he decides to send them out there.'

'What do you intend to do then?' She was troubled but she made no effort to get him to change his mind, accepting what he said instantly.

'I'll check in at the hotel and scout

around, see if I can discover the exact tie-up between Gruber and those outlaws.' He let out his breach, slow and easy. There was no doubt in his mind that this was not going to be as easy as it sounded and danger would be his constant companion until these renegades had all been run to earth. But for that to happen, he needed help; help from all of the decent folk in the town and surrounding ranches. As yet, he saw no way in which he would get that much-needed help. Somehow, he had to find a way to overcome the natural fear of these people, make them see that, together, they could defeat Gruber and his hired gunslingers.

He waited while the girl rode out of town. At the far end of the dusty street she paused for a moment, threw a swift glance behind her, waved one slim arm, then disappeared towards the trail, which led back to the ranch. He paused for an instant, then gave the sorrel its head and trotted the animal to the livery stables. A tall, gangling youth came out, thin and bony with the look of a boy who has little good meat in him. He seemed awkward, tongue-tied, as he took the sorrel.

'Better let him cool off a little before you water and feed him,' advised Steve quietly.

He handed over the reins, seeking the other's confidence. 'I hear that there ain't a sheriff in Twin Buttes. Any idea what happened?'

The boy flashed him a quick look, evidently liked what he saw, for he went on confidentially. 'The last three were shot by outlaws. Nobody wanted the job after that. Can't say I blame folk.' He lowered his voice still further and glanced about him before adding: 'They do say that Bart Gruber is determined there ain't going to be another sheriff of Twin Buttes, unless he puts him in office himself. Then he'd be running the town.'

'Funny,' said Steve. 'I got the impression he was running things right now.'

'He is, but right now, it doesn't show.' The boy led the sorrel away and Steve ladled a long, refreshing drink of the cool water from the bucket which hung above the well in the courtyard. It came to him that what the other said was so obviously true that it could well have been missed by most of the townsfolk. Gruber had worked his way into this position so insidiously that few people must have realized it before it was too late to do much about it. Bleak-eyed, he went in the door of the hotel and walked towards the desk. The clerk, small and weedy-looking, eyed him shrewdly, taking in the dusty, travel-stained clothes and the guns hung low. He tightened his lips into a thin, hard line.

'I'd like a room,' said Steve shortly.

'How long do you intend staying?' There was no mistaking the antipathy in the other's voice.

'I haven't quite made up my mind yet,' said Steve casually. 'I've got some unfinished business to attend to in Twin Buttes. Once it's finished, I'll ride out of here, not before.'

The other pursed thin lips. 'Could be that it'll be dangerous around these parts for a man like you,' said the clerk pointedly. He slid the register towards Steve, waited until he had signed his name, then glanced down at it, turning it towards him. Steve noticed the change in the other's expression instantly.

'Oh – Mister Yarborough. We have a room all ready for you. I'm sure that you'll find it comfortable and to your taste.'

'You were expecting me?' Steve eyed the other in sudden surprise.

The clerk gave an ingratiating smile, turned and took a key from the metal rack behind him, and lifted a flap, moving around the end of the desk. 'Mister Gruber said we were to expect you this morning. He had an idea you'd be staying in town for some time and he arranged this room for you.' He led the way up the stairs which, even though the sun was shining brilliantly outside, seemed to be dull and gloomy, filled with shadows in every corner. Throwing open one of the doors along the wide corridor at the head of the stairs, the clerk stood to one side and allowed him to enter.

After he had gone, Steve walked over to the window and opened it, sucking in deep breaths of the hot, dry air that swirled above the street, baking in the sun of high noon. The clerk's original hostility did not bother him any more. His body felt punished by that long morning ride and he was conscious only of the mind's ache of memory, of the ranch-house he had seen, burned to the ground, everything in it destroyed, of the two people, dead and possibly soon to be forgotten and the ache was something which would not be blotted out or smoothed away by lesser, physical pains.

The room was small, facing the front of the hotel, looking out on to the main street of Twin Buttes and even though he had thrown open the window to its fullest extent, it still held the day's heat and dust. He rolled a smoke, lit it absently and was then suddenly motionless, staring across the street at the window in the building on the opposite side, the long match burning out between his fingers as his keen gaze caught the sudden, swift flicker of movement there. The next instant, acting on an impulsive instinct which had saved his life many times in the past, he threw himself back into the room, away from the window, diving for the floor. The sharp, vicious crack of the rifle was loud in his ears as he hit the floor with a smashing impact which knocked all of the wind out of his body and sent a sharp stab of agony lancing up his arm and into his chest.

The bullet burned through the air where his head had been a split second earlier and buried itself in the plaster of the opposite wall. He rolled over a couple of times, then slowly edged himself to his feet, the heavy Colt balanced in his right hand, his finger bar-straight on the trigger. He risked a quick glance towards the shadowed window from which the would-be assassin had fired that shot. There was no movement there now and reluctantly he jammed the gun back into its holster.

Mister Gruber has arranged this room for you.
The barbed words stuck in his thoughts and there was no way for him to tear them loose. No wonder Gruber had been so anxious to choose this particular room for him, so that his hired killer might have the chance of shooting him down in cold blood. For the first time, he realized the kind of a man he was up against.

His lips drew back in a mirthless grin that showed his teeth. Why had he not expected something like this? He had made his attitude quite clear as far as Gruber was concerned and the other knew that he represented a definite menace that would have to be removed – and fast, if he was to remain in a position of power here. This town wasn't big enough to hold the two of them. There was no way of telling how often something like this had happened to some unsuspecting rancher. Down in the street, there was no sign that the shot had been heard, or if it had, these people knew by now that it was safer and wiser to mind one's own business.

Stretching himself out full length on the low, iron bed, he clasped his hands behind his head, staring up at the ceiling above him, trying to marshal his thoughts into some form of order. Most of Gruber's men, he guessed, would be swaggering killers and braggarts easily handled because their actions were always predictable, but not so Gruber himself. A man as dangerous as a coiled rattler, who could strike in several ways. Once he discovered that his first attempt at murder had been a failure, he would try again. And as before the attempt would be made by stealth.

But he would not make the attempt yet. In the meantime, it was essential that he should make some plans of his own. There were a lot of things he did not know, a lot of loose ends lying around which tied in somewhere. Those renegades who haunted the desert, striking at the wagon trains, evidently working hand in hand with Gruber. Did they ever ride into Twin Buttes to get their orders from this man who owned most of the surrounding territory? If they did, obviously they came by night. They would never dare to enter town in broad daylight.

Outside in the street, life seemed to be proceeding normally. There was the sound of horsemen riding slowly into the town and the lilting melody of a tinkling piano from the saloon across the street.

Gradually, the laughter grew low, the noise

of the piano faded and there was silence outside, as the shimmering heat of the afternoon lay over the town. He felt as though he could sleep, but he knew that this could be dangerous. It was dark when he finally rose, the gnawing hunger pains in his belly, and went down into the lounge. Going out into the street, he made his way across to the saloon, pushing open the swing door and stepping inside, eyes alert. There were several men at the bar, and in one corner, a small, sad-faced man, wearing a hat a size too large for him, was running his fingers aimlessly over the piano keys, pounding out some old, half-forgotten song that spoke of a time before war and death, of a pleasant time when the sun was warm and the breezes soft and the desert through which he had ridden on his errand of vengeance was far away.

Several card games were in progress at the tables, but he ignored these, trying to pick out any men there who might be in the pay of Bart Gruber, and in particular any who looked as though they might have been crouched behind a window a few hours earlier, squinting along the sights of a high-powered rifle. A knot of men were gathered at the far end of the bar and he saw them turn as one man, to run their eyes over him. Tough, grim-visaged men who wore their guns low. Hired gunslingers, he thought tightly. No doubting whose men they were.

There was now an icy coldness in his brain, washing away everything else. He could smell trouble here, not yet sure from which direction it would come, or when it would break. There was no sign of Gruber. He would know by now that he had failed to have him killed and he had probably already given the orders to his men. Thinning his lips, he stepped towards the bar, glanced sharply at the barkeep who was watching him out of faintly frightened eyes. For a single, tense moment, it was as if all sound and movement in the large room had been sheared off by a machet. Then the pianist began playing again as he felt the eyes of the gunslingers at the bar on him.

The barkeep pushed a bottle towards him, then a glass. Steve filled the glass slowly, keeping his eye on the reflection of the gunslingers in the huge crystal mirror at the back of the bar. Behind him, he saw the batwing doors open again and a man came in, a tall man with a cruel, hawk-like face and piercing black eyes that swept around the room before finally fastening on Steve's back. He came forward with a thin, sneering grin on his face, standing a few yards behind Steve, his legs spread slightly apart, his hands not very far from his guns.

'You still in Twin Buttes, Yarborough?' said the other thinly.

Steve turned very slowly, eyes slitted. He deliberately unfocused his gaze, taking in every move made by the bunch of gun-slingers at the far end of the bar, knowing instinctively that as soon as this man made his play, they would join in. Quite obviously, this had been set up by Gruber and he was taking no chances this time.

'You figuring that I ought not to be here?' he demanded harshly.

The other shrugged his shoulders negligently. 'Seems you've been doing a lot of talking to Mister Gruber that he doesn't like, Yarborough. He reckoned you might have taken the hint and ridden out of town this afternoon while you had the chance. A pity that you didn't.'

The reptilian gaze locked with Steve's, then flickered away for a brief second in the direction of the men at the bar. A fast man with a gun, thought Steve tightly, just looking for an opening to draw on him. Not that the other would have to justify any law in Twin Buttes and wait for Steve to draw first. But there was still a little public opinion to be taken into account and not all of the men in the bar were Gruber's friends.

'You sure seem mighty anxious to pick a quarrel with me, stranger,' said Steve easily. Deliberately, he went on: 'Could it be that you tried before with a rifle? This afternoon.' He spoke derisively now, goading the other, hoping to prompt him into action.

The slitted orbs glinted in the light from the chandeliers. The fingers were clawed above the gun-belt. But still, the other made no move to go for his guns. He stood there in a half-crouch, eyes never once looking away from Steve's face. 'I mebbe missed you once, cow-poke,' he said sneeringly. 'But this time, I've got you here and I don't intend to make the same mistake twice. You're as good as dead, Yarborough. Gruber has given orders that you ain't to stay alive. You been asking too many questions that he doesn't like.'

'Seems to be that Gruber has good cause to be afraid. If you intend to die for him, then make a play for your guns or get out.' Without turning his head, Steve said crisply: 'And as for your friends at the end of the bar, if they want to be in on this deal, they can go for their irons too.' There was a hardness in Steve's tone which brought the others bolt upright, where they lounged against the wide bar.

'You damned fool,' spat the gunman harshly. 'You seem mighty anxious to die.' There was a smooth purr to his voice, a kind of hypnotic quality, but Steve had the unshakable impression that the other wasn't quite as sure of himself now as he had been when he had first walked into the bar. Maybe in the past, he had come up against men like Steve and shot them down in cold blood, thereby earning his reputation as a killer. Perhaps those men had fled town rather than face this killer's guns and had been shot down on the trail.

The tension and the silence drew themselves out until the atmosphere in the bar became almost unbearable. Very slowly, the killer edged his way forward, circling Steve a little as he stood against the bar, his arms hanging loosely by his sides, eyes not moving from the other's face, watching for the first sign which would tell him when the other intended to make his play. He saw the faint filming of sweat which had formed on the gunslinger's brow. The other was obviously depending on his friends at the end of the bar to make their play at the same time as himself.

Then, suddenly, with a snarled oath, his hands flashed downward with the speed of striking snakes. Steve laughed soundlessly. His hands did not seem to move very quickly, but the guns had leapt into them as if they had possessed a strange form of life all their own. The hammers slammed down and in that tenth of a second before the two slugs tore into his body, the killer knew that he had met a man much faster than himself. The other's sixguns clattered to the floor of the bar a second before his body crashed on top of them. In that same second, there came the flicker of movement from the end of the bar as the other killers tried to go for their guns, fanning out to take Steve from two sides, presenting more difficult targets. Steve's third shot was directed, not at the killers, still bunched together, but at the single chandelier hanging in the centre of the wide ceiling. The bullet parted the metal chain holding it there and it crashed down on to the floor, the lights being extinguished instantly.

There were thin screams from the women in the room as they tried to get clear of the gunplay. The brief stabs of orange flame from the guns on the other side of the room, gave away the positions of the other killers. Steve went down on one knee, heard the hum of bullets passing over his head in the darkness. His own guns roared, bucking in his hands. He fired instinctively at the direction of the muzzle flashes, heard one man utter a low groan of pain as a bullet hit. The glass behind the bar shattered with a weird splintering sound which almost attracted his attention away from what was happening in front of him.

He slitted his eyes against the stabbing flashes of the weapons, his ears protesting at the savage thunder of sound in the confined space, the echoes reverberating around the walls. He was not baffled by the sharp explosion of the guns or the smell of cordite fumes in his nostrils. Somebody yelled a few yards away as he crawled forward, head down. Now he could see a little in the dimness, saw two shadowy figures that tried to leap forward behind the cover of an overturned table. The guns in his hands spoke again and one of the figures moved forward a little, then stumbled, pulling the table over on top of him as he went down, a bullet in his chest.

He sucked in a deep breath and steadied

himself. This was a little more than he had really bargained for. He had not intended to take on so many of Gruber's men at the same time, but now he was fighting for his life. He knew that he could expect no help from any of the other men in the saloon. They had seen too much happen in the past to risk their lives helping him, they had lived too long in the stranglehold which this man had on the town and the surrounding area. He gripped his guns hard, scuttled to one side as bullets crashed all around him, finished up near the bar. There was no sign of the barkeep. He had probably taken the opportunity of getting out as fast as he had been able to move, once he had seen the trouble brewing up. A tall, vaguely-seen figure rose up from behind one of the tables.

'This is where you get it, Yarborough,' snarled a harsh voice from another direction. A bullet ploughed into the floor less than two inches from his leg. He fired swiftly and instinctively, not in the direction from which the voice had come, but at the dark figure that moved swiftly, trying to slide across his vision while that sudden voice distracted him. The man coughed hoarsely, slid down on one knee, the gun clattering on to the floor. Then he rolled over, out of sight and there were only two stabbing flashes of flame coming at him from two different directions. He grinned mirthlessly in the darkness. Now he knew exactly where those two killers were. Three had been killed, together with the first man to challenge him. If he succeeded in killing these two gunslingers, it was just possible that he could get the people of this town, the decent folk, on to his side and form them into a coherent whole, capable of joining with the smaller ranch owners against Gruber. Even then it would be a hard and uphill fight, but he had the feeling that it would be worth it, even if it only meant that a girl like Sarah Tennant and her father might be allowed to live in peace, and not have to face every night with the fear that the ranch might be burned to the ground around them by a band of outlaws.

He gazed into the smoke that swirled and eddied about him, eyes narrowed, watching for the slightest movement. He could sense the crush of men around him and could hear the thump of his own heart keeping an uneven rhythm in his chest with the breathing of the two remaining killers who seemed intent now on stalking him down from two different directions, possibly hoping to confuse him and take him from two sides.

A bullet hit the top of the table close beside him, and a second later, another cut into the floor in front of him. He wriggled forward in the dark, felt his outstretched hand touch something soft and yielding. His fingers explored it for a second before he realized that it was the killer's body, the face still frozen into that mask of stunned surprise. Edging his way sideways, he froze and strained his ears to pick out the slightest sound which might tell him where the other killers were. For a long moment, there seemed to be no sound in the bar. He held the Colts tightly in the palms of his hands, hammers at full cock, jerking them up as flame spat at him from the far corner of the room.

His answering fire was immediate and accurate. He heard the bullets thudding home, caught the wheezing sigh as the man slumped forward. He moved again, stealthily, going forward now, around to his right where he guessed the last gunslick to be, crouched behind one of the tables. He caught the slither of sound as the other moved uneasily and he got the impression that the man was transferring his weight from one foot to the other, possibly that he was reloading his guns.

'Better make your play, killer,' he said softly, throwing himself to one side the next instant.

There was a breathless pause, then the other's gunfire split the room. The bullets went wild. Evidently the other was jumpy, knew that the rest of his companions were dead and that he alone was left to face up to this man who seemed able to see in the dark and whose shots rarely, if ever, missed their targets. More shots came from the other, still aimed wildly. A bullet ricocheted along the whole length of the bar, smashed into the splintered pieces of the mirror still in place, bringing more of the glass down.

Seconds later, sighting swift and sure, Steve fired. The guns were literally torn from the other's grasp as the bullets struck the guns, spinning them out of the man's hands. Steve had fired deliberately to disarm the other. He needed one of these killers alive. He had to find out the answers to some questions and if Gruber wouldn't answer them himself, then this seemed the only other way to get them.

Pouching the guns, he hurled himself forward, throwing his body between two of the overturned tables. The killer, knowing that Steve had the drop on him, turned to run for the batwing doors. He had moved less than three feet when Steve caught up with him, grasping him by the shoulder, swinging him round heavily and crashing a bunched fist into the other's face. The man staggered back over one of the tables, then kicked upward with his foot instinctively. The move took Steve completely by surprise. The other's booted heel caught him full in the chest. He felt his shirt rip as the rowel of the spur was dragged along the cloth and something scraped along his flesh.

Instinct made him roll away from the boot which lashed downward at him as the other, quick to seize his advantage, tried to kick in the side of his skull. He was on his feet a moment later, saw the other moving in swiftly. Deliberately he smashed his bunched fist twice into the other's throat. The killer cursed with a wheezing grunt and reeled back, arms flailing in front of his face as he tried to fight back. Steve, sucking in air into his raw throat and heaving lungs, forced himself to move forward, to give the other no chance to get back on balance. Three hammer-like blows sent the other reeling drunkenly against the wall where he remained, arms hanging limply by his sides, all of the strength and fight gone from his body. His jaw hung slackly open and his eyes were almost closed. There was a streak of blood on his cheek where Steve's fist had grazed the skin.

Carefully, Steve turned to survey the saloon behind him. Now that all of the shooting was over, someone brought in candles and in the flickering light, it was possible for him to make out the bodies of the dead men lying behind the tables and the killer who had first challenged him in the middle of the floor. The barkeep was back behind the bar, stepping gingerly over the splinters of broken glass, eyeing Steve with a new respect.

There was a sudden movement outside and the batwing doors were thrust open again. Steve's hands cleared the guns from leather again, instantly on the alert, but the two men who came in, looking about them in surprise, did not seem to be Gruber's men. He relaxed as they came over to him. One man, tall and grey-haired, with a long, drooping moustache, held himself erect with what seemed like a military bearing. He eyed Steve tightly, then glanced to where the last gunman leaned against the wall, shaking his head to clear it, the blood still oozing down his cheek. The level gaze flicked back to Steve.

'What happened to this one, stranger?'

Steve shrugged. 'I figured I might need one of those gunslingers to give me a few answers as to why they jumped me like that.'

'Could be.' The other nodded, eyed the dead men on the floor grimly. 'Gruber isn't going to like this one little bit when he finds out what's happened. But I reckon one thing's for sure. You have a cast-iron alibi, you must have shot in self-defence. Nobody in their right minds goes single-handed for six gunmen.'

'That won't make much difference as far as Gruber is concerned; if he brings along that deputy he's managed to swear in, he'll do everything he can to get me thrown in jail on a charge of murder.'

There was a tight, grim bitterness in Steve's voice as he went over to the bar and picked up the bottle of whiskey which seemed somehow to have survived all of the shooting. He poured himself another glass and threw it down his throat in a single gulp. It brought some of the feeling back into his bruised body.

The grey-haired man came over and stood

beside him. 'I'm Doc Manston,' he said quietly. 'I'd like a word with you in my office in, say, half an hour's time. It's important.'

'All right,' Steve agreed. 'If I'm still at liberty.'

The thick brows were lifted for a moment, then the other said confidently. 'I reckon you will be. Gruber still has to pander a lot to public opinion, until he's more sure of himself. He doesn't want the whole town to rise up against him. If it does, he knows that he'll lose. He'll have to wait until he's brought in a few more hired gunmen. He'll still be planning to kill you though, so watch your step.'

'I'll be careful,' Steve promised. He leaned against the bar and watched as the other man strode out with the short, silent man close on his heels. Inwardly, he wondered what the other could possibly have to say to him that was so all-fired important. Whatever it was, it seemed certainly something he did not wish everyone in town to know about.

In spite of the shooting, Gruber did not put in an appearance at the saloon, although Steve did not doubt that he knew of it, knew what had happened, that he had not only failed again, but that six of his best men had been killed and there was another who had been taken alive. A man who could be doubly dangerous because he might talk; and there was little doubt that this was the last thing that Gruber wanted. Steve looked across at the defeated gunman, saw the sullen eyes stare at him for a moment, saw the anger and intense hatred in their depths, knew that this man would kill him the first opportunity that he got. He had been humiliated in front of the townsfolk and that was something he could never forgive.

'Reckon you'd better come with me,' said Steve harshly, prodding the other with the barrel of his Colt. 'Doesn't look as if Gruber is going to show his face here and get you out of this.'

Unwillingly, the other got to his feet and stumbled towards the door. His face still looked a mess from the beating he had taken and he trailed one leg a little behind the other. Out in the street, there seemed to be nobody on the boardwalks, but Steve had the feel of eyes watching him, unfriendly eyes, and knew that there were men in the shadows. He felt the tightening of his stomach muscles as he urged the other forward. It was only a little way to where he had spotted the doctor's place on his first ride through the town with Sarah Tennant that morning.

'Where d'you think you're taking me?' demanded the other thickly, after a moment's silence. 'This ain't the way to the jailhouse.'

Steve grinned harshly. 'You didn't think I'd take you there, did you?' he drawled, 'so that Gruber's man could free you the minute I turned my back?' He shook his head. 'I think we'll pay a call on Doc Manston. Seems he has something to say and he may know of ways to make you talk.'

'I ain't saying nothing,' muttered the other stubbornly.

'You'll talk,' promised Steve, 'and fast. May interest you to know that I learned a few Indian tricks a while back. They're guaranteed to make any man talk. So don't be too sure of yourself.'

'You'll pay for this when Gruber hears about it,' snarled the other savagely as Steve thrust him up on to the boardwalk at the corner of the deserted street. 'You don't think that Gruber is going to let you get away with this, do you?' There was a definite trace of fear in his voice now, which had been missing before. He was no longer so confident that everything was going to be all right for him. This man who had killed six of his companions and who held a gun in his back at that very moment, was undoubtedly a tougher proposition than the local ranchers who had ridden into town breathing vengeance on Gruber.

There was a light in the window of the small office and surgery and Steve prodded the gunman towards the door. Once he got this man to answer a few questions, he would know where he stood.

He knocked loudly at the door. A moment later, it opened and the grey-haired man stood in the opening. He motioned them inside, showed no surprise when he saw Steve's companion. In fact, reflected Steve, it was almost as if he had been expecting the other.

The man who had been with Doc Manston inside the saloon, lounged against the far wall, the grey eyes not once leaving the small group of men in the room.

'Sit down, Yarborough,' said the doctor, motioning towards a chair. 'No need to keep your eye on this character, not as long as Adams is here with me. He'll shoot to wound if this *hombre* makes one wrong move. You brought him here to try to question him, I presume.'

Steve nodded as he lowered himself gratefully into the chair. 'I thought he might be persuaded to talk, to tell us all that he knows, particularly about the set up that Gruber has in this town. More than anything else, I want to know where Gruber fits in with those outlaws in the desert out there to the east.'

The doctor rubbed his chin thoughtfully, eyeing the gunman speculatively. He nodded finally. 'We'll get him to talk, never fear,' he said quietly. 'But first, the business I wanted to see you about. It may come as a surprise to you, and you're quite at liberty to refuse what I'm going to ask you. In fact, if you're wise and want to live to a ripe old age, you will turn down my proposition. But after seeing what happened back there in the saloon and knowing what kind of a man you are, I think I'd be more than justified in offering you the vacant post of sheriff of Twin Buttes.'

For an instant, Steve felt certain that he had not heard the other aright. It seemed impossible that these people should want him as their sheriff. They scarcely knew him. He had been in town less than twenty-four hours and yet, already, he was being offered this job. The other seemed to take his silence for fear, for he went on quickly:

'I know what you must be thinking, Yarborough. The last three sheriffs we had were shot down in cold blood by the renegades, although we never did get the men who did it. They rode out of town and headed into the desert and that's where they are right now. So far as we know, they never showed their faces in Twin Buttes again.'

Steve forced a smile. 'It isn't that, exactly. It's just that I'm so overwhelmed. You know little about me and yet you offer me this job.'

'We need a man who can handle his guns and in particular one who can stand up to Gruber. He's trying to get one of his men into the post. Then he'll run this town just as he wants it. We have to have a man here of our own choice. You seemed to me to be the logical choice. At least, we'll know that you can't be bought over by Gruber. I don't know what it is between you two, and that's your business entirely, so I ain't aiming to pry into that. But there isn't much time for you to think it over. Gruber will do every-thing in his power to stop you from being elected and we have to be ready for him.'

'We?' asked Steve tightly. 'Do you honestly think that the people in this town will ever band together and rise against Gruber and his men, even though they know that he's behind all of these senseless killings?'

The other's shoulders sagged for a moment. 'I suppose not,' he admitted finally. 'They would take a whole heap of convincing and even then, it's difficult to be sure.'

'That's what I mean. What good is a sheriff unless he has the people firmly behind him? It doesn't seem to me that it could ever work out.'

'I understand. It was just an idea I had to help the town. If we don't do something soon, Gruber will have taken over completely and then everything will be finished. We'll never get another chance.'

Steve's mouth set in a determined line. He fingered the butts of his Colts for a moment with curved fingers, aware of the other's eye on him, watching him carefully. 'Do you honestly reckon that it would help if I accepted the post of sheriff?' he asked tightly.

The other glanced up again, a flicker of hope in the deep-set eyes. 'I'm sure that it would. It would be dangerous as far as you were concerned. I won't hide that fact from you, but you strike me as a man who has met danger many times before and in many guises, and always been able to face up to it and overcome it.'

'That's true, perhaps. And what if Gruber doesn't like this idea of yours, of putting me forward as sheriff?'

'He won't,' affirmed the other. 'But I reckon we must cross that bridge when we come to it.' He crossed over to where the gunman stood sullenly against the wall.

'Now what did you want to know from this character?'

Steve walked forward and stood in front of the other. 'I want to know how and when Gruber gives his orders to that outlaw band in the desert and also where their hideout is.'

The man's lips set themselves into a narrow line across the middle of his hard features. 'You don't think I'd tell you that even if I did know it, do you?'

'I think you will.' Doc Manston went over to the table, slid open one of the drawers and took out something smooth and slender that shone in the overhead light. He came forward and held it out to the gunman. The blade of the wicked-looking scalpel glinted bluely in the light and Steve saw the sweat suddenly pop out on the other's face and begin to trickle down between his eyes. He licked his lips drily, his Adam's apple jerking up and down convulsively.

'They come to see Gruber at midnight. I don't know when, they never say when they'll come, but he always seems to know.' He swallowed thickly.

'And where do they have their hide-out in the desert?' persisted Steve. 'I want to know that exactly. Draw me a map of the area if you have to.'

'That's something I don't know.' The other suddenly jerked out the last word as the tip of the scalpel touched the skin of his throat and went in a little way, drawing blood. He muttered softly under his breath, trying to hold his head well back. 'For God's sake take that thing away,' he rasped. 'I'll tell you all that I know. They have their hide-out over the river and—'

The glass in the window splintered into a thousand fragments. Steve heard the bark of the rifle a split second after he saw the gunman pitch forwards at his feet, the blood beginning to spread from the wound in his chest.

5

THE DESPERADOES

Swiftly, without pausing to think, Steve leapt for the window, bringing up the gun from its holster in a smooth motion. Outside, the street was quiet. There was no sign of the man who had fired that shot, but one thing was certain in Steve's mind, it had been one of Gruber's men, one who had followed them from the saloon with orders to make sure that the gunman did not talk. Reluctantly, he lowered the gun and went back to the others. Doc Manston was bending over the man stretched out full length on the floor. He remained there for a moment, then got slowly to his feet, glanced round in Steve's direction, and shook his head quietly.

'He's dead, I'm afraid,' he said harshly. 'We'll get nothing from him. Did you see anything out there, any sign of that killer?'

'Nope.' Steve's voice was hard and brittle. 'He must have been hiding out on the far side of the street just waiting his chance. Too dark out there now to see anything and we wouldn't stand a chance of tracking him down now. He'll probably be back at the saloon, or holed up with that coyote, Gruber, giving him all of the details. A pity, because I reckon this man could've told us a lot.'

Manston nodded. His face was tight and serious. He went over to the desk in a corner of the room and lowered himself into the chair behind it, elbows resting on the polished mahogany top. 'Now do you see why we need a man like you here, Yarborough? We need a man who isn't scared of these rats, who can stand up to them and more important still, who can outdraw Gruber's hired killers. You probably heard what happened to the last three men we had as sheriff. All of them shot down in cold blood. Sure it was made to look like a fair fight in every case, but that fooled nobody.'

'I see your point,' Steve agreed. 'But like I said before, what good is a sheriff if he can't get the backing of decent, honest men, if he can't form a posse and know that they'll stay at his back in spite of everything that Gruber will do? One man can do nothing against this nestful of snakes.'

140

'I know,' muttered the other. He grew serious and kept glancing towards the splintered window. 'But you're our only hope now. If you can stand against Gruber, show him that you intend to be sheriff, even though you may have only the two of us to back you at first, I'm convinced that the ranchers and townsfolk would back you in the end.'

'By the time they came around to that way of thinking you and I could be dead.' Steve told him harshly. He paused, stared down at the dead man on the floor and let his thoughts drift through his mind for a long moment. The dead man was an outlaw, just like those in the desert, and even though he had died violently at the hands of one of his erstwhile companions, Steve could feel no pity for him. He could not shut out of his mind and memory the men and women on that wagon train in the white, moonlit wastes of the desert, with the red-bearded giant, Madison, firing until his last bullet, in a vain effort to stop the massacre. And later, there had been that small ranch-house, razed to the ground on Gruber's orders, in spite of his protestations of innocence.

Perhaps it was this that decided him. Looking back on it later, he could not be sure; but he found himself nodding slowly. 'If you figure I can do anything as sheriff, I'm willing to give it a try.'

'Good.' The other stood up quickly, opened one of the drawers in front of him and brought out something which glittered in the light from the lamp. He came around the edge of the desk, up to Steve, and pinned the star on to his shirt. 'This makes it official,' he said quietly. 'Not that Gruber is going to like it. He'll do everything in his power to get this declared void, but as he well knows, we have the right to elect the sheriff. We represent the citizens of Twin Buttes.'

For a moment, Steve stared down at the badge on his shirt, feeling a strange sense of unreality. It seemed impossible that these people should have chosen him as sheriff, particularly since he had just killed five men back there in the saloon. By rights, if Gruber had his way, he would be inside the jail by now, awaiting trial on a charge of murder.

He glanced across at Doc Manston. 'When do you figure that Gruber will make his play?' he asked, and his voice was as cold as his words.

'Soon,' was the reply. The grey-haired man

stood near the table. 'But I reckon that first we had better get rid of him,' he nodded down towards the body of the gunman on the floor. 'By now, I guess that Gruber knows what happened back there in the saloon. He'll be over there now, trying to swear in a lot of the roughnecks to form a posse and hunt you down, and you can be certain that there would be more of his men there tonight, ready to swear that you drew first and the others merely had to defend themselves. You'll have been branded a sure-fire killer by now, Yarborough.'

Steve smiled thinly, touched the handles of the heavy Colts, almost caressingly. 'I'm ready for 'em as soon as they come,' he said defiantly. 'I reckon it's about time I took up residence in the sheriff's office. If they want to know where to find me, they'll soon find out.'

He stepped towards the body on the floor, then paused. There was shouting outside, the noise coming from somewhere further along the street in the direction of the saloon. Dimly, he could hear the sound of booted feet on the boardwalk. 'Sounds like we've got trouble already,' he muttered coolly.

'They're coming here,' said Manston

warningly. 'That killer must have told them.' He gestured sharply towards the thin-faced man, but the other was already moving, melting into the shadows near the window, a gun sliding swiftly into his right hand.

'No gunplay,' warned Steve tightly. 'We'll hear what they have to say first. Then if they still want trouble, they shall have it.' He eased the Colts once or twice in their holsters, then stood in the centre of the room, with his hands hanging loosely by his sides. The sound of the rabble grew louder as they came surging along the street. They stopped outside the door and an instant later, he heard Gruber's voice, calling to them to be silent. The crowd obeyed instantly.

A moment later, Gruber's voice yelled: 'You in there, Manston?'

'I'm here, Gruber. What do you want? Why bring that crowd of hellions snarling at my door at this time of night?'

'You got that killer Yarborough in there?' A hard voice, demanding answer, with the threat lying just beneath the surface. 'If he is, I want him out here. He shot down some of my men in cold blood back there in the saloon. I've got plenty of witnesses here, enough evidence to hang him.'

'I'm here, Gruber,' called Steve loudly, not moving an inch. 'Trouble is that we have one of your boys here and he can testify plenty too.'

'Fool talk, Yarborough,' snapped the other. 'You can't bluff me like that. He's dead and he can't–'

Steve strode swiftly to the door, jerked it open, stood there, staring out at the others. Gruber stood in the middle of the street, looking up at him. 'How d'you know that he's dead?' snapped Steve harshly, 'Unless it was you, or one of your hired killers who pulled that trigger.'

For an instant, there was silence in the street. Gruber stared up at him with hate showing clearly in the deep-set eyes. He stepped back a pace. 'You trying to say that I had him killed, Yarborough?'

'That's right. To make sure that he didn't talk. And as for those witnesses you have behind you, ready to say that I pulled on those gunslingers in the saloon first, their word means nothing as far as this town is concerned.'

Gruber's lips drew back in a thin, mirthless smile. 'You're suddenly a hard man, Yarborough. What's happened to make you this way, I wonder?'

145

Before Steve could answer, Doc Manston pushed his way forward and stood on the edge of the boardwalk, eyes snapping as he glared down at the bigger man. 'Reckon I can answer that for you, Gruber,' he said, and his voice was even and calm. 'We've had a talk and decided that with so much lawlessness in the town it was time we elected ourselves a new sheriff. And with the power invested in us, we went ahead and did that.' He jerked his thumb towards the star on Steve's chest, a badge which Gruber seemed to notice for the first time. 'And here's the man we elected sheriff.' He paused for a brief moment, then went on deliberately, 'And I reckon you'll find it a little more difficult to get rid of him as you did the others. He won't be so easy to shoot in the back.'

'Just what are you insinuating, Manston?'

'I'm insinuating nothing,' retorted the other. 'I'm just saying what everybody in this town knows.'

Gruber's hand moved swiftly, poised above the gun in his belt, froze there as Steve's voice rasped: 'Hold it right there, Gruber. I'm just itching to kill you, and I will if you make a further move for those guns.'

For a moment, it was as if Gruber intended to go through with his attempt, in spite of the warning he had got. Then he relaxed, moved his hands away from the guns, until they hung limply by his sides. He shrugged his shoulders with a negligent gesture. 'So you figure on making this killer the sheriff of Twin Buttes, Manston. I always reckoned that you had more sense than that. You don't think the rest of the townsfolk are going to back you in this foolishness. They won't stand for having a killer as sheriff.'

'Could be that they'd sooner have him than one of your hired gunmen,' snapped Manston tightly. 'You're only scared because you figure that he might be able to get some of these people to take a stand against you and when they do, you'll find that the town ain't big enough to hold you and your kind, and they'll either kill you or run you and your men out of town.'

'Nobody gives me orders, or makes threats like that to me, Manston,' snarled the other harshly. He walked forward a couple of paces. 'I'm the one who gives the orders around here and don't you – or this sheriff you've elected – forget that. Just because you pin a star on a man don't mean to say that he'll lead a charmed life, or that he gets the right to give me orders.'

There were angry mutters from the men in the street behind him and Steve narrowed his eyes, watching the men closely. They were nearly all men who rode with Gruber and they were in an ugly mood. There were only three men against more than twenty and he knew that if it came to a showdown right here, in the street, he and the two men with him stood little chance of outshooting all of these men. Then he relaxed as he saw Gruber turn sharply on his heel and stride off down the street. Ten yards away, he paused, turned: 'You ain't heard the last of this, Yarborough. They may have made you sheriff, but you won't live long, I promise you that.'

The night was cold and the air smelled clean and fresh after the stale, hot smoke and noise of the saloon. Steve rode slowly through the foothills with the small posse behind him. There were seventeen men with him, including Doc Manston, men he had picked out of the hotel and saloon and who had agreed to ride with him, not to hunt down Gruber, but to try to pick up the trail of the outlaw band operating in the desert to the east. They rode with him, Steve knew, because they did not expect him to locate this renegade gang. Had he asked them to ride with him against Gruber, they would never have agreed to do so.

They followed the rising curve of the hill. The moon had risen and was still low in the sky and over their heads, hung the night's big silence. As he rode, Steve felt the grim determination grow within him until it was something so huge that he could scarcely contain it. Perhaps he had brought these men out here on a wild goose chase, but there was a little thought running around in his mind which refused to give him rest. If his ideas were right and these outlaws were working hand-in-glove with Gruber, then they had to come into Twin Buttes to get their orders, or Gruber had to ride out to them. Somehow, he doubted if Gruber was in the habit of riding off into the desert in search of these renegades. And now, at this moment, there were urgent things Gruber would have to discuss with them. Steve Yarborough was the sheriff of Twin Buttes and that could spell trouble for everyone concerned. So the first thing to do, if Gruber wanted to retain his position of power there, would be to rid the territory of

Steve Yarborough; and what better way of doing that than to have the outlaws carry out the dirty work.

He thinned his lips into a grim, unseen smile in the darkness. The thought of vengeance was a stirring thing deep within his mind, something which gave him no peace. He sat tall in the saddle, a man loaded with threat in every movement, equal to the task which faced him, unsure only of the men who rode with him. Would they fight when the time came, or would they drop back and leave him to ride on alone? It was something he did not know as yet. Once they crossed into the alkaline wastes of the desert, he would find out.

By morning, they had reached the very edge of the desert where it stretched clear before them to the sun-shimmering horizon. The whiteness of all that alkali hurt the eyes if they looked on it too long and Steve deliberately averted his gaze after a few moments' keen speculation. The river was shallow and sluggish as they paused on the western bank.

'You figuring on taking the men across there into that wilderness, Steve?' asked Manston, reining his mount close to Steve.

The other shook his head. 'Ain't no sense

moving out into the desert. They won't hide out in there. They'll have some place among the rocks on the border. That's where we'll find them. I guess our best chance is to look for tracks along the river. They'll have to come down here some time for water. Ain't much in the hills.' His keen eyes turned to the other. 'You think these men will follow us?'

Manston shrugged. 'I'm not sure. They still seem eager to ride with us, but could be that's because they figure you'll never find these outlaws. If they thought there was a real chance of that, they might turn their mounts and pull out. They're not cowards, but they have wives and children to think of and they see no real reason why they should risk their lives just because you want to even the score with the men who attacked that wagon train.'

Steve sucked in his lips. 'For God's sake, can't they see that as long as this band is allowed to operate, nobody is safe? Take care of these renegades, and we've destroyed half of Gruber's power.'

They kicked their horses, weary now after the long night's ride east and cut through the rocks and brush that bordered the river. Two hours later, they reached the small

151

stream that Steve recognized as the one which ran past the small homestead he had seen burned down. They reined their horses here for rest and drink. Impatiently, Steve sat high in the saddle, peering about him with slitted eyes. The sun was high and already the heat was cutting through his shirt with a fiery, stabbing touch.

'Reckon we ought to rest here ourselves,' suggested Doc Manston quietly, with a quick nod towards the rest of the men, sitting weary and travel-stained in their saddles. 'It ain't wise to push these men too far, not at the beginning anyhow, Steve. They'll follow you right now, but soon they're going to get around to asking themselves why they're out here on this trail that seems to lead them nowhere and once they start talking like that among themselves, they'll cut out and head back to town in spite of anything you say.'

Steve lifted his brows into a bar-straight line. 'Those men have been sworn in as deputies,' he said, his voice harsh. 'They'll ride with me as long as I say so.'

The other shrugged his shoulders. 'You sure must hate these outlaws to act this way,' he said solemnly.

'I do,' acknowledged the other. He

paused, then went on: 'Still, I guess a couple of hours won't make much difference and these horses are beat. We'll camp here until the afternoon, then head north again. Those renegades are sure to be somewhere in this area. If only we can pick up their trail.'

There was dust and heat all around them as they dismounted. Steve's smile was gone now and his eyes were cold as he looked around at the men, squatting on the ground near the stream. 'Doc here reckons you're all figuring on us not meeting up with these outlaws,' he said thinly. 'I figure that we'll pick up their trail some time this afternoon. They're around here some place and I intend to find them and when I do, I want every man in that gang either dead, or a prisoner. You all understand that?'

There were low murmurs from the men, but they nodded their heads slowly and reluctantly. One of them said harshly: 'How many d'you reckon there are in this band, Sheriff?'

Steve pursed his lips. 'Hard to say. I saw only twenty when they attacked that wagon train and we must have killed seven or eight of them during the fight. I'd guess there are probably ten or a dozen left, unless more have joined them in the meantime. We ought to outnumber them two to one. And I picked you men because they told me you were all handy with your guns.'

There was challenge in his words. Challenge that waited for a definite answer from these men. He saw them staring down at the ground at their feet, not looking at him.

'Look,' he said thinly, 'Gruber has been running this place long enough now. You've knuckled under to him because you're afraid that he'll burn down your homes, rustle off your cattle, and if all that fails to get you out of the territory, then he'll send his men to kill you. Most of this you've brought upon yourselves. You've let him carry out these murders without lifting a hand to stop him. You've had three lawmen chosen by yourselves, and when they were shot down in cold blood, did you avenge their deaths, did you try to find the men who pulled the triggers that killed them? No – you tried to fool yourselves into thinking that if you let things go on the way they were going, everything would turn out all right in the end. But Gruber isn't satisfied with what he's got. He wants more, a lot more. Not until he owns every foot of ground in this territory is he going to stop these killings.

And by that time, he'll own you all, body and soul.'

One of the men shook his head slowly. 'There's a lot more to this than you know about, Sheriff,' he said hoarsely. He shifted uneasily, 'You've been here for only a little while. You don't know Gruber as we do. He has a hundred men at his back, outlaws, gunslingers, men wanted for murder and robbery in half a dozen states, with a price on their heads. But so long as they ride with him, they're safe from the law – and they know it. Make no mistake, they'll fight if he gives the order. Do you expect us to stand up to an army of hired killers like that? We aren't professional gunmen like they are. We're ordinary men, ranchers, shopkeepers, gamblers, and cowhands.'

Steve thinned his lips. 'You've missed one thing,' he said deliberately. 'If this country is ever to grow up, if there's ever to be law and order here, then it's going to be because of the efforts of men like you, not killers like Gruber. This fighting and destroying won't last for ever. The railroad will come through here soon. The stage line is here already. Things are going to start moving soon and it'll be the ordinary men and women who'll make it come.'

They were silent at that and Steve did not press them any further. He knew with an instinct deep down inside him that they would follow him now. Doc Manston, sitting close beside him, said softly: 'All of that sounds as though you're sorry you brought some of these men out with you on this vengeance trail.'

'I'm not sorry,' said Steve evenly. 'What I did when I picked these men, I'd do again. But I don't mean to let anyone slow me down on this gang hunt. I'll track down these outlaws, Doc. I'll ride right through to their hideout and—'

'All hell won't be enough to stop you.' Doc Manston finished the other's sentence with a serious laugh. 'I understand what's driving you like this, Steve. Sometimes, vengeance can be a terrible, soul-destroying thing. But I'll admit that in this case, it's necessary. We have to stand and fight some time and if you're the man who's going to make us do it, then the sooner we get it over with, the better.'

Steve gave them two hours, then motioned them back into the saddles. They swung up wearily. After riding all night, with eyes straining into the moonlit darkness for the first signs of danger, knowing that the outlaws knew this country far better than they did and could strike from ambush without warning, there had been no let-up of that tension which had grown within every man since they had ridden out of Twin Buttes. Steve wondered if Gruber had watched them ride out and if so, if he knew why they had left, a posse of men riding east, evidently seeking trouble, especially with the tall, hard-faced man riding in their lead. If he had seen them head out and had guessed at their intentions, they had seen no sign that he was following them. Presumably he had already warned the outlaws that they could expect trouble from this man who had been newly elected sheriff and he considered that the outlaws, forewarned, could take care of themselves without any additional help from him.

He felt the muscles tighten under his ribs as he leaned forward in the saddle, eyeing the ground ahead of him, staring down for the first sign of tracks in the soft ground. Among the rocks, there would be no chance of picking out a trail, but here, close to the water's edge, the ground was sufficiently soft for any hoofmarks to show. It was hard riding, in the heat and the dust, monotonous and mean. But Steve forced the others on, even when they seemed on the point of turning back. Somewhere, he argued, there must be a place where the outlaws came down to the water. That was something they could never do without. And he doubted if they ever went to the extent of trying to rub out their tracks. They would not have considered the possibility that anyone would be so foolish as to ride them down on their own territory.

A sudden shout from one of the men jerked his head around. He gigged the sorrel, rode forward quickly. The man pointed with his right hand. The trail led down to the water's edge and then back up into the rocks, where it was no longer visible. Steve nodded, satisfied. 'That's their track, all right,' he said sharply. 'Think we can follow it through the rocks?'

The man threw a swift glance in the direction of the towering boulders which lay to their left. He shrugged non-committally. 'Could be,' he admitted grudgingly and then went on: 'But it won't be so easy among those rocks. Hoofprints won't show well there.'

They turned their horses and cut into the rocks, eyes alert, moving from side to side, ready to pick out the spot where a single print showed in a patch of open ground among the rocks. They entered a long canyon that stretched away to the north-west, running between towering cliffs, so that they now rode in shadow in spite of the fact that the sun was still near its zenith. It was old to Steve, this tracking down of a bunch of killers. His keen-eyed gaze took in every sign which lay in front of them. Here and there, a bush had been trampled down and branches had been snapped off others which seemed to grow out of the very rock itself, where life fought for a hard and precarious hold in this barren, terrible land. The signs were all too clear to his probing gaze. The trail was fresh, had been made in the past day or so. But as they rode, he felt the tightening sense of apprehension in his chest. They could be moving into big trouble, warned a little voice at the back of his mind, a voice which he had learned from past experience never to ignore. The outlaws, if they had been warned by Gruber, would be on the look out for them, might even have spotted them already and if so, the first intimation they would have of their presence would be a hail of gunfire from the rocks. It was for this reason that he lifted his head at frequent intervals to scan the rocks above them, eyes slitted against the glare of sunlight reflected from red sandstone, probing the narrow crannies and boulders for anything which moved, for the telltale glint of sunlight striking the metal of a rifle.

They reached the end of the gully and came out into more open country. The mountains were still around them, but the peaks seemed to have receded a little on all sides and here, where the scrub grew up tall around the trail, the danger of ambush was increased. Steve whirled in the saddle, motioned the others to keep close to the trail. Doc Manston urged his horse forwards, rode up beside him, his face bearing a serious expression.

'You think there's trouble ahead, Steve?' he asked tightly, eyes flicking from side to side.

'I'm sure of it,' nodded the other. The muscles of his jaw lumped under the skin as he turned his head slowly to take in the whole scene around them. 'If only we could–' He broke off suddenly, pointed.

The solitary rider was so far distant that it was pure chance that Steve had seen him. Had he been looking straight at him, it was conceivable that he would have missed the movement on the horizon completely, but with averted vision, his keen eyes caught the movement, swung a little and held.

Manston gave a quick nod, shaded his eyes. 'Who do you reckon that is?' he muttered harshly. 'Whoever he is, he's heading this way fast. Must be in some hurry to get some place.'

Steve watched the rider for a moment, then shook his head quickly. 'He isn't heading this way,' he said. The contour of the ground told him clearly that the man was swinging north a little, along a trail which would carry him far over to their right. Why? The answer came to him a moment later. 'That's one of Gruber's men,' he said. 'Probably heading towards the outlaw hideout to warn them about us. I could have been wrong when I figured that Gruber had already warned them. Whoever that is, he's using an old trail.'

'One thing's certain. He hasn't seen us yet,' said Manston. 'What do you figure on doing now?'

'Only one thing we can do. This means that the outlaws won't be expecting us to be paying them this visit. We'll have to reach them before they know we're here. Once that rider warns them, they'll have every man out watching the trail. If we can get there and hit them before they're ready for us, we stand a better chance. Besides they may decide not to fight when they see how many men we have and I don't want a single man to get away.'

'They can't be far away,' mused the other. 'Not many places where they could hide out around here.'

'Do you figure they'll fight?' queried Steve softly. His face betrayed no sign of the thoughts that were racing through his mind.

'They'll fight,' said Manston emphatically. 'They'll fight – and if they aren't killed, they'll hang.'

They urged their horses into motion. The rider on the horizon had vanished now among the low foothills in the distance, but there was still a cloud of dust hanging in the still air, kicked up by the flying hoofs of his mount.

'Do you know this country?' Steve asked the man who rode beside him.

'Ridden it once or twice,' said Manston. 'That other rider must have used the old Indian trail across the prairie to the west. Comes out close to the Tennant place. Say, you don't think it could be Tennant? That old fool is just as likely to try to settle these things himself as stay behind out of trouble.'

'It ain't likely.' Steve didn't like to admit that possibility, even to himself. If it had been Tennant riding hard towards the hideout of these renegades possibly filled with a burning desire to bring some form of justice by himself, then things could flare up with an unexpected fury. Half an hour passed and then an hour as they rode deeper into the foothills. They were still following the trail which led down to the river, thereby setting Steve's mind at rest. It seemed to him that these men had made their hideout a long way from water. It was the best part of ten miles to the river and they had passed several places which looked as though they could have been turned into good hiding places by this gang.

They were almost on top of the others before Steve realized that danger was so close. His eyes had been watching so closely for the trail they had been following that he had failed to notice that they were among the rocks again, the character of the terrain had changed abruptly and they were no longer in the open ground. The smell of a wood fire, drifting on the air, touching his nostrils, rang the warning bell in his mind. His hands pulled hard on the reins, bringing the sorrel to a standstill. His right hand lifted as he signalled the rest of the men to stop. It needed only one horse to snicker, to make a sound and they would have been discovered. But there was no sound. Gently, the men eased their mounts back along the trail as Steve signalled them away. They checked their horses on the leeward side of a low rise which looked forward into the rocks where the thin coil of black smoke lifted to the clear blue of the heavens.

'How many are there?' asked Manston in a tight whisper. 'Did you see?'

Steve shook his head. 'Very likely they are all here,' he said. 'but I couldn't be certain.' He pointed off to the rocks which lay in front of them, a little to one side of the trail. 'We'll move into position there,' he said softly, so that not a single word carried beyond the group of waiting men. 'Leave the horses here. And remember, no shooting until I give the signal. I want to take these men by surprise.

A moment to check their guns, then Steve led them forwards, waving his arm to spread the men out. They were not old hands at this game, and he was still a little worried in case one of them pulled the trigger of his gun before he gave the signal and spoiled everything. He could see that they were jumpy, all except Doc Manston and the thin-faced man who looked like a professional killer, but seemed to have thrown in his lot with them. He could be relied upon to keep cool and handle his guns to good account.

Very slowly, Steve edged his way forward among the rocks. Once, he heard the sound of a spur striking an outcrop of stone and the sharp sound trembled along his nerves while he waited for what seemed an eternity, holding his breath, releasing it only when there came no sound from where he had seen the outlaws. The scent of the wood fire was strong in his nostrils now. He heard the voices of the men a moment later as they talked around the fire. Voices that spoke harshly together as they listened to the man who had ridden out from the town to warn them of a danger which was even closer than they had anticipated,

Very carefully, he lifted his head, stared down at the scene in front of him. There were twelve men around the fire, one of them he recognized instantly as the man he had seen lounging outside the sheriff's office in Twin Buttes the day he had ridden into the town, the man who had claimed he was the deputy there. Gruber must have entrusted this mission to him, ordering him to ride at full speed to warn the outlaws of their danger. There was a stand of brush not far from the fire and it was to a rope stretched between this and the pile of rocks thirty feet or so away, that the horses were tethered. Steve let his gaze wander over the horses speculatively. If he could get them away before the renegades could reach them, they would be trapped there and forced to fight. He motioned Doc Manston and the thin-faced man towards him. They scrambled over the rocks in silence, breathing heavily as they came up to him, sweat showing on their faces.

'We've got to get rid of their horses,' he said in a hoarse whisper. 'I don't want them to be able to ride out of here.'

'That isn't going to be so easy,' muttered the thin-faced man. He nodded to the string of horses and Steve saw, for the first time, the man seated on one of the rocks, a rifle across his knees, a thin wisp of smoke rising from the cigarette in his mouth. A man who watched warily, obviously alert to danger.

Tightening his lips, Steve swung a quick glance around the hideout. On the face of it, it seemed impossible for anyone to get close enough to those tethered mounts to stampede them after cutting them loose. And the first shot which killed that guard, would warn the others. There was just one chance if he could entice that man away into the rocks which lay immediately behind him. He turned and whispered instructions to the two men, then slithered away into the sun-blistered rocks, feeling them hot under his hands. Cautiously, he worked his way around the outlaw camp, passing one or two of the posse on the way. The men eyed him curiously, nodded in understanding as he spoke quietly to them. They went back to their places, leaning against the rock, guns in their hands. Time was running out, thought Steve tightly as he slipped into the rocks directly behind the watching guard. The horses jerked and pulled at their reins a few yards away to his right, uneasy, possibly sensing the presence of the other horses, tethered over the rise, even though they could not see them. The guard too, seemed uneasy, throwing swift, apprehensive glances over his shoulder. For a moment, Steve glanced up against the glaring sun, at the places where the rest of the men were hidden among the rocks, then tore his gaze away with some reluctance. He ran the tip of his tongue over his lips, crouching down in the partial shelter of the rocks, fingers of his left hand feeling around for a fair-sized stone. They closed over one a moment later and, still keeping low, he tossed it into the air, into the boulders three feet from where he lay, his right hand gripped around the barrel of his gun. This would have to be done in silence if the plan was to work. The stone clattered among the rocks and out of the corner of his eye, he saw the guard start to his feet, staring around him, lips tightened in the sweat-lined face. There was no sign from the men clustered around the wood fire that they had noticed anything wrong. Very slowly, Steve eased himself back into the shadows among the rocks and waited. The man was still wary; his rifle left behind on the rock, his sixgun in his hand. In spite of the stiffness in his limbs from the long ride, Steve moved catlike among the rocks, making no sound as the man came closer. The other kept twisting his head, peering in every direction, even behind him at times, eyes flicking from side to side, warily, probing every shadow round him for anything that moved.

There was little time to think. As soon as he judged that the man was sufficiently far into the rocks to be invisible to the men seated around the fire, Steve acted. At any moment, he knew, the outlaws might begin to post their men on look-out, to watch the trail for their approach, and they would spot the horses within seconds of climbing those rocks. Gliding forward like a ghost, Steve brought the Colt up like a club. For a moment, it was poised above the other man's head. Then it crashed downward, striking the back of his skull with a sickening, hollow sound. Steve caught the other's body as he slumped forward and eased it down among the rocks. There remained only a few minutes before the man's absence was noticed.

Swiftly, he slithered around the rocks, circling the clearing, until he came up to the rope which held the outlaws' horses tethered together. It was the work of a few seconds to slice through the rope which had been tied to a short stake driven into the hard ground at the base of the rocks. The other end, Steve knew, tied to that brush, would snap within seconds when the strain of twelve stampeding horses came to bear on it.

Satisfied, he moved back into the rocks, emptying his lungs in a sudden sigh. So far, everything had gone without hitch, but now came the tricky part. Judging the distance nicely, he waited until he was well out of range of those horses when they stampeded, then he pulled out the Colt and fired three shots low over the necks of the horses. They were already uneasy and skittish, and the shots, echoing back from the rocky walls, were enough to turn the trick. The nearest horses reared savagely, thrashing with flailing forelegs at the rope which now held them only at one point. As Steve had judged, it gave within seconds and bucking and rearing, the mounts stampeded towards the open country.

6

A THUNDER OF GUNFIRE

The crash of other shots sounded a second later in sharp, angry counter to the thunder of the running horses. An instant and Steve had crawled forward through the rocks until he was looking out directly upon the men clustered around the fire. For a brief fraction of a second, they stood there, on their feet now, staring out at the rising cloud of dust which almost obscured the retreating shapes of the horses. Then the tall, hard-faced man whom Steve remembered so well, the leader of the men who had attacked and massacred everyone but himself on that wagon train, uttered a sudden bellow of bull-like anger, clawed for the guns at his waist and dived for the ground to one side, firing as he went down out of sight.

Steve drew in a deep breath, slitted his eyes against the sunglare, and fired a couple of quick shots at the place where the man had dropped under cover. The bullets hammered off solid rock and went whining away into the distance, in murderous ricochet. Guns flared in brief, stabbing flashes of flame as the other men among the rocks, having waited for his signal, joined in. Two of the outlaws lay dead around the fire. Neither had had a chance to pull his gun before the bullets had hit. They lay face downwards in the sunlight, arms stretched out in front of them, almost as if they had been pegged out there by Indians, in the sun, to die.

A hail of bullets struck the rocks around Steve as he threw himself back into the hollow beside the unconscious body of the guard. His position was known to almost all of the outlaws and unlike the other men in the rocks above, his position there was precarious. It was possible for the outlaws to rush him as he lay there and even a hail of bullets from above might not be sufficient to stop them.

Savagely, filled with consuming anger, he fired two more shots into the rocks where the outlaws lay hidden. Gun thunder echoed along the narrow valley as the outlaws fired back desperately, knowing themselves to be trapped. They had chosen

172

this place, supposing themselves to be safe from an attack from any source. Steve smiled grimly to himself among the rocks, keeping his head low as the slugs flew over his body. They had overlooked, however, the fact that it might be possible for a posse to come upon them without any warning, as had happened now. If they had had their men posted among the rocks, to watch every trail leading into the area, they would have seen them in time, but with this man riding in from Gruber, they had neglected to take this elementary precaution.

'You don't stand a chance,' Steve yelled suddenly, without exposing his position. 'Better give yourselves up and come out with your hands raised. I promise you'll all get a fair trial.'

'That's what you say,' snarled a harsh voice from somewhere among the rocks. 'We know what kind of trial we'll get in Twin Buttes. A rope from the nearest tree. If you're wanting to take us in, come and get us.'

'This is your last warning.' Steve lifted his voice to be heard above the gunfire. 'You don't stand a chance, you're completely surrounded and your horses are miles away by now.'

The outlaw leader laughed harshly. The sound of it echoed out into the rocks. He was keeping himself well hidden and Steve tried desperately to locate the position from which that harsh laugh had come, but it was impossible. With an effort, he edged to one side, sliding between the rocks. Reaching the end, he fired savagely, guns alternately pumping and bucking up and down in his hands.

For a moment, the firing from the outlaw camp slackened and he lunged forward to hit the ground ten feet further on, diving for cover. He reached it and lay still for a moment, pulling air down into his heaving lungs. A couple of shots whined close to his head as he tucked it down behind the rocks. He was now less than twenty yards from the fire. There was no sign of the other outlaws, except for the two bodies lying in the streaming sunlight. How many others had been hit, it was impossible to tell, but he guessed that some of them had been, from the way they had gone down under cover.

Swiftly, he rammed fresh shells into the chambers of the guns. A smashing volley crashed out from the positions among the rocks overhead. The men there, possibly led by the thin-faced man with Doc Manston, were moving in now, their fire more concentrated and accurate than before as their bullets found their mark. Steve came back into the fire just as the first of the men reached the bottom of the rocks and crouched down out of sight. One glance was enough to tell him that they were surrounding the outlaw camp and their bullets were finding their mark as they placed their shots with effective precision.

Carefully, Steve lifted his head until he was able to peer between the scrub on top of the boulders. In the distance, on the far side of the fire, he could just make out Doc Manston and a handful of the other men, snaking their way forward through the long grass, throwing lead as they advanced. One man fell, clawing at his throat in his death throes, but the others kept on, driven forward by Doc Manston. Now there was nothing to stop them. Steve threw all caution to the wind, rose to his feet and advanced towards the outlaws, guns flaming in his hands as he went forwards. He made a perfect target as he walked forwards, but there was something about him, something terrible and avenging that seemed to strike terror into the hearts of the renegades. A slug laid a red-hot brand along his left arm and there was a tensed feeling inside his body like that of a coiled spring waiting to unwind. Shots came from among the rocks and the outlaws were pulling back now towards the entrance of the cave which led away into the rocks.

'We've got them on the run.' Doc Manston's voice reached Steve as he ran forwards. One of the outlaws, hard-eyed and stony-faced, rose up from behind the rocks, both guns held tightly in his hands. Steve fired instinctively, saw the man stumble forwards, clutching at his chest. The mouth slackened, the eyes began to turn upward, the guns dropped from dead, nerveless fingers, two bullets cutting into the ground as the man went down. An outlaw screamed as two slugs smashed into his shoulder. The gun flew from his fingers as the shattering impact swung him round, knocking him on to one knee.

The outlaws pulled back into the rocks which lay scattered around the entrance of the cave cutting back into the rocks. Once in there, he knew, they would be shooting from excellent cover and it would be difficult to prise them out. He told Manston and a bunch of the others to move to the right, to cut the men off. For a moment, his attention was distracted from the rocks directly in front of him. He caught the flicker of movement in the same instant that instinct prompted him to throw himself to one side, the gun in his right hand jerking against the wrist. The bullet plucked at his shirt and the blow of striking hard ground knocked all of the wind from his body. Even as he fell, he saw the tall shape of the outlaw leader rise up from the rocks, run forwards, bringing up the gun to cover him. Deep down inside, he knew that he could not hope to bring his own gun to bear in time, to prevent the other from squeezing the trigger which would blast him into eternity.

'I'm going to kill you, Yarborough.' It was simply said, but there was venom at the back of the quiet words, each one carrying the promise of death. The gun came up inexorably until Steve found himself staring down the barrel with the outlaw's finger tightening on the trigger. The hammer went back, the brilliant light was visible in the killer's eyes. Then the hammer snapped forward as he squeezed the trigger and clicked on an empty chamber. Anger and frustration showed on the other's face as Steve pushed himself swiftly to his feet, moving forwards at the same time, head low, knowing that he had little chance in which to use his own gun, that he had to hit this man, and hit him hard, before he could recover.

Savagely, the other swung downward with the gun, cursing harshly, the breath rasping in his throat. The barrel struck Steve on the shoulder – there had been no time for the other to reverse it and use it as a club – and he felt the metal of the gunsight rip the cloth and bite into his skin, drawing blood. The sharp pain which lanced through his chest and shoulder acted as a spur to Steve. He kicked savagely with his feet, caught the other on the side of the leg, hurling him to one side. Still the other held on grimly, jabbing at his throat with a bent elbow. Sparks flashed in front of Steve's eyes and for a moment it was as if every muscle and nerve in his throat and chest had been paralysed. He tried desperately to suck air into his heaving lungs. There was a red haze floating in front of his vision and he shook his head savagely in an effort to clear it.

For a moment, he lay there, with the air sighing harshly and noisily in and out of his constricted throat. A frantic rhythm jabbed at his senses. The outlaw uttered a savage bellow of rage and came in again. His blurred face drifted in front of Steve's vision. Breathing through his open mouth Steve forced himself to clear his vision, lashing out with his bunched fist at the grinning, leering face in front of him. With a feeling of solid satisfaction, he felt his fist strike home, felt something give. The other reeled back against the rocks, spitting blood where some of his teeth were missing. Now he was a fighting, snarling animal. When he came in again, leaping from the rock, propelled by his legs, he roared with rage. A fist came out of nowhere and caught Steve on the face, knocking him backward, but he felt nothing, no pain, no feeling. Anger rode him now, spurred him on, made him able to disregard all pain. He threw his body backwards as the other lunged in, saw the outlaw stumble, grabbed for the foot which came for his stomach as the man fought to regain his balance, twisted savagely, feeling the weight behind the foot lift and turn as he applied all of his strength. There was a thunderous roaring in his ears and a throbbing pain at the back of his forehead, and a curious crackling sound that he failed to identify.

For a moment nothing happened and he became aware that the other man had not moved, that his body was limp. Gradually, his vision cleared and he could see properly again. The outlaw leader lay at his feet, his body twisted over the rocks at a strange, grotesque angle. That last fall had caught him in a wrong position and had broken his back. With an effort, Steve pushed himself upright, stood swaying for a moment, aware of the shouting in the distance and that odd crackling sound which seemed to be originating from somewhere close at hand although he could not make out what it was.

There was a dizziness in him still but he forced himself to keep his eyes open, to stare about him, before picking up his gun from where it had fallen. Then he saw what the noise was, even as Doc Manston came running towards him.

'Steve! Quickly over here.' It was difficult to see the other as he ran forward, gun in his hand. Behind him, there was a dark cloud that reached up until it almost blotted out the sun. And at the base of it, the red-tongued flames which ran swiftly in all directions, clawing at the long, brown grass, now as dry as tinder.

To Steve, it was as if time stood still. With a physical effort, he made his feet move. Already, the fire had spread across almost fifty yards at the head of the clearing and lay between them and the horses. It was clear what the outlaws intended to do, put up this screen of flames between themselves and the avenging posse. There was danger here too. If the outlaws, those who were still alive, succeeded in keeping them cut off from the horses, they might decide to make a try for them themselves.

Ignoring the pain in his body and the smoke that brought tears to his eyes, making it difficult for him to see properly, he ran forwards, felt hands catch hold of him, dragging him over the uneven ground, with the flames roaring in his ears. He felt the heat on his face with the shock of a physical blow. Then they were through and crouched down with the others.

'How many men did we lose?' Steve asked thickly. He wiped the sweat from his face with the back of his hand.

'Four dead,' said Doc Manston evenly. 'Two have got bullets in their shoulders, but they'll live once I get them back to Twin Buttes.'

'And the outlaws? Anybody see how many are left?'

'Couldn't be more than half a dozen,' said one of the men. 'Five of 'em are dead out there and you killed one yourself.'

Steve nodded. He threw a swiftly probing look in the direction of the cave mouth, now almost entirely hidden by the flames and smoke. What little wind there was, unfortunately, seemed to be taking the fire away from the cave and towards the point where they lay. A few ragged shots broke from the cave and lead spattered the boulders around them, forcing down their heads.

'Those few that are still alive,' said Steve with a touch of amusement in his voice, 'there don't seem to be much wrong with their aim.'

'They know we've got them trapped. Reckon they'll try to break out of there soon. They're probably hoping that the fire will drive us back far enough for them to be able to make a break for it.'

The thin-faced man, the professional killer who had somehow thrown himself in with the law, was calmly lifting bullets from his belt and feeding them into the guns. When he had finished and every chamber was filled to his satisfaction he sat there in the rocks and awaited developments.

Steve said quietly: 'They can't wait in there much longer. Sooner or later, they're going to have to try to get out and reach our horses.' He turned to the doctor. 'Any of our men back there with them?'

'A handful. They came down from the rocks on the far side of the cave, to surround those renegades. I reckon they'll be holed up there among the boulders ready for anything like that.'

'I only hope you're right,' Steve muttered fiercely. 'If they get through to the horses, we're finished.' He eased himself forward until he lay on the very edge of the rocks, where he could see the whole stretch of ground in front of him.

'All of you men are trapped in there,' he called loudly, raising his voice so that his words might carry above the ominous crackle of the flames. 'Throw out your guns and come on out. I'll still see to it that you all get a fair trial. Your leader is dead. He won't be able to help you any more.'

'Save your breath, lawman.' The voice of the deputy he had met earlier came to him out of the wreathing smoke, a vicious snarl of sound. 'We know what kind of trial we can expect if we surrender to you. A lynching at the end of a rope thrown over the nearest convenient tree. I've seen it happen too many times in the past to believe you now.'

'It's the only chance you've got. The wind's changing. Pretty soon, you're going to be caught in a trap of your own making.'

'Go to hell, lawman.' There was a pause, followed by an orange stab of flame from the cave mouth as the outlaw fired at the sound of his voice, but Steve had thrown himself to one side and the bullet droned harmlessly by through the scrub.

Swiftly, Steve fired a couple of shots into the smoke in the direction of the muzzle flash. He thought he heard a sudden grunt of pain, but with the harsh crackling of flames near at hand, it was impossible to be sure. For a long moment after that, there was silence; a deep and uneasy silence in which Steve strained his ears to pick out any sound. He could make out nothing through the smoke, although it was certain now that the wind had changed and was driving the flames back in the direction of the cave mouth. He had little idea of how far that opening extended back into the solid rock face, but it could not be far enough to afford much shelter to those outlaws trapped there if the fire did reach the entrance. Taking careful aim, he fired two more shots into the swirling smoke. A man cried out in agony as one of the slugs struck an invisible target.

Another pause, longer than before. Steve slitted his eyes against the sunglare and waited. Then the same voice yelled: 'One of our men has been hit, Sheriff, he's bleeding to death. We need help.'

Beside him, Doc Manston made to move forwards, but Steve caught his sleeve and held him back. 'It's a trap,' he said thickly. 'Just stay where you are, Doc. They're just waiting for you to get up and make them a present of a target and they'll drop you.' Aloud, he called: 'All right, all of you, come on out of there and we'll take a look at him.'

For a long time, there was no movement, no sound, then that harsh, sneering voice said: 'How do we know that you'll keep your word, that you won't shoot us down in cold blood as soon as we show ourselves?'

'You don't. That's a risk you'll have to take. There are a lot of men here who'd give anything to shoot you down like you did a lot of others. But we'll hang you legally, if it comes to that.'

'All right, we'll come out. Just see to it that those trigger-happy men with you hold their fire.'

Steve waited, keeping his eyes on the smoke which filtered across the opening in the rock. He could just make out a short,

185

shadowy figure, moving forward with hands held high. For a moment, he relaxed. 'Looks like they mean it,' he said softly to Manston. Loudly, he called: 'All right men, hold your fire. Looks as though they're coming out.'

The man emerged from the smoke, shuffling his feet in the sand, moving very slowly as if he had been wounded. Out of the corner of his eye, Steve saw the thin-faced man a few feet away, lift himself slightly, the guns in his hands, pointed straight at the figure emerging from the smoke. There was a moment's anger inside him. Undoubtedly, the other was deter-mined to shoot this man down, and the others who followed him, even though they had asked to surrender. He turned to bark a command at the other, cursing savagely under his breath, then stopped, whirled swiftly at the sudden commotion in the cave mouth, a commotion only faintly and dimly seen through the obscuring cloud of smoke. The man who had been shuffling forward, as though wounded, had stopped while still just inside the smoke. Even as Steve turned his gaze on him, the man's hands suddenly dropped to the guns which were still in the holsters at his waist.

Several of the men in the posse had already

risen from their hiding places and were holstering their guns, waiting for the outlaws to come out and give themselves up. These men were caught off balance. They were not prepared for what was going to happen. The outlaws had never intended that they should surrender. It had all been part of a trick and he, Steve Yarborough, had been green enough to fall for it. The shadows of the other outlaws, running forward, with their guns blazing as they ran, showed through the smoke. But already, the thin-faced man, his eyes hard and glittering under the wide brim of the hat, was loosing off round after round. The leading man who had sprung the trap, his hands still clawing for the guns in the holsters, fell forwards on to his face in the charred and blackened grass. Savagely, Steve pushed himself to his feet. There was no fear in his mind now, only a burning anger at the way he had been fooled and the manner in which he had jeopardized the lives of all of the men with him. The guns in his hands jerked swiftly as he advanced on the men, rushing through the smoke, turning as they came out of it and heading in the direction of the tethered horses, where there was little opposition. Bullets ripped and sang through the air. Some ricocheted off the solid rock, but others found their mark in soft, yielding flesh. Two more of the outlaws stumbled as they were hit. One turned, guns still gripped in his hands as he tried drunkenly to bring them to bear on the men who strode avengingly after him, bringing up the weapons with a painful slowness as if they were too heavy for him to lift. The eyes, turned towards Steve, were glazing over, the muscles of his face relaxing. Then his knees sagged beneath him and he flopped forward on to his face in the dirt. His fingers, out-stretched on the burned grass, clawed themselves into tight fists as he died, then relaxed slowly.

Grunting with the effort, Steve moved purposely forward after the rest of the outlaws. There were only four still on their feet and they came between two streams of fire as those men with the horses, warned by the shooting, opened up with their weapons. It was all over in less than five minutes. When the firing died, all of the outlaws had been killed. Not a single man had sur-rendered, they had all preferred to die with their guns in their hands, to die in violence as they had lived.

Going back to the fire which was slowly burning itself out, as the flames beat futilely against the rock, Steve came once again upon the body of the outlaw leader. He turned the man over and stared down into the cruel, pitiless face which held an expression of sullen surprise, even in death. He sighed, pouched the guns and relaxed. There was a great weariness in his body, but a lot of the bitter ache had evaporated. He lifted his head and stared round at the others, grouped in a tight little bunch, their faces glistened in the sunlight.

'I don't think we'll have any more trouble around these parts,' said Steve tightly. 'Reckon those wagon trains from Freeman City will be able to go through unmolested from now on.'

Doc Manston stood looking down at the body of the man Gruber had put up for deputy. He lay on his back, eyes staring sightlessly at the blue mirror of the sky where the smoke from the fire was gradually beginning to fade. 'Reckon Gruber is going to be pretty mad when he hears about this,' he said solemnly. 'Could be he'll decide to take things into his own hands, call out all of his men for one big showdown. He can't afford to let this go unavenged. Once the townsfolk and the other ranchers hear that his outlaw friends have been shot down and wiped out, they might take it into their heads to rise against him and if they do, things might be a little too even for him. He'd prefer to wipe us out before we can get any help from them.'

Steve nodded. That made sense. 'We'll head back for Twin Buttes,' he said quietly. 'If Gruber is expecting us to have been routed by these men, he may be off balance when he sees that we somehow made it. I want to keep things that way, if possible.'

Doc Manston nodded wisely. 'We could head back by that old Indian trail through the foothills. It will cut off about five miles of the trail.'

'Then lead the way,' said Steve sharply. 'You know this part of the country.

They went over to their horses, swung themselves up into the saddles, kicked free the ropes which tethered the animals. Slowly, they rode out of that place of death, leaving four of their own number and more than a dozen of the outlaws as buzzard meat in the burned grass. No need to keep the tightness in his mind now, reflected Steve as he rode behind Doc Manston. He had fulfilled his vow, had brought death to the man who had annihilated every other man and woman and child on that doomed wagon train.

Night reached in from the east and they were still inside the scrubland which lay to the east of the arable cattle country around Twin Buttes. All of the men were travel-weary now and those who had been wounded during the gun battle, slumped forward in their saddles, every movement sending a lanced barb of pain through their bodies. But Steve, acting on a strange impulse that he could not define himself, kept them moving long after it was dark. Even though there was no hope of reaching the town for more than seven hours, he continued to urge them forward until it became obvious, even to him, that they would have to rest up and camp for the night and continue the ride the next morning.

There was no need of a fire here. The night was warm and it would have served to give away their presence there to any rider belonging to Gruber's band. Better to eat the jerky beef they carried in their saddle pouches and sleep in their blankets in the total darkness, than to give away their location.

For most of the night, Steve Yarborough

slept soundly, but he woke once and sat up in his blankets, straining his ears in an attempt to pick out that sound which had penetrated to the part of his brain which never slept, waking him instantly, warning him that something was wrong in the velvet darkness which lay over the prairie. He sat like that for several moments, trying to locate the sound again, but for a long while, there was nothing. A coyote wailed with a mournful, dismal howl somewhere in the distance and seconds afterwards, the sound was echoed from another direction. But coyotes had never wakened him before and he knew that it was not that which had torn his mind from the exhausted sleep into which he had fallen the moment his head had touched the ground.

Then dimly, in the distance, many miles away to the west, he picked out the sound again. The faint drumming thunder of horses on the move; a lot of horse-flesh, and moving fast. Whoever was out there was in a mighty hurry and was driving those animals to the limit. For a moment, he considered the possibility of a cattle herd on the move, possibly even a stampede, then put the idea out of his mind. It wasn't that, he felt certain. He had heard the terrifying sound of a thousand head of cattle on the move, too many times in the past to mistake it now. These were horsemen, riding hard and fast, and he knew, by some hidden instinct, that they were not out there on any errand of mercy. The only men likely to be moving at that early hour of the morning, were Gruber's men. The thought flashed through his mind, worrying him more than he cared to admit. Just what were those men doing out there? Whose ranch were they burning this time, whose cattle were they rustling, driving south to the border, or holing up in some secret part of the range, ready for Gruber whenever he had time to alter the brands?

He half rose to his feet, glanced about him in the darkness, saw that none of the other men was awake. All were rolled in their blankets and their even breathing told him that none had been wakened by this sound. Uneasy in his mind, he settled back into his blankets. The riders were too far away for them ever to hope to catch them even if they saddled up and set out right away. By the time they covered all of that distance, the men would be back in Twin Buttes and there would be no proof to use against Bart Gruber. The other was far too clever to give the law any chance to pin murder or rustling on him. When he woke again, it was almost dawn. The air was clear and sweet and he drew great breaths of it down into his lungs. Getting to his feet, he rolled up the blanket and strapped it into place on the sorrel. There was a driving impatience in him now. That sound he had heard during the night still itched in his brain and although he tried hard to tell himself that perhaps nothing was wrong, he did not believe it for a single instant. Gruber's men never went out riding in the night unless it was to burn and pillage and destroy. His eyes were cold as he went over to where the other men sat together, eating the thin strips of jerky beef, washing them down with the cold, clear water from their canteens. Some of the men made themselves smokes, but he urged them on to their feet.

'Saddle up, men,' he said harshly. 'Time we were moving out.' He caught Doc Manston's eyes on him, eyes which held a look of curiosity, and he motioned the other forward, saying in a soft tone. 'There was something happening during the night. Riders over to the west, about five miles or so, I reckoned. Could have been Gruber's men out riding. If they were, I think we ought to get back to town as soon as possible. I'd like to know what he's doing right now.'

'You think he could have known what happened yesterday, and he's getting ready to meet us in Twin Buttes?' For the first time, Steve noticed the look of alarm in the older man's eyes.

'It's possible.' Steve said no more, but swung himself quickly and easily into the saddle. The rest of the men did likewise, the wounded, their shoulders bandaged as well as could be expected, taking more time. 'Let's move out,' he called thinly. 'Keep your eyes open for any sign of Gruber's men on the trail.'

The sun rose behind them as they rode out of the scrubland, into the tall, lush grass of the cattle country. As they rode, anxiety and an uneasy worry grew in Steve's mind. He could not put out of his thoughts the feeling that something had happened during the night, something terrible, which would not have occurred if he had not been out hunting down those outlaws. He felt sure that he had ridded the territory of one evil, only to have let another, more terrible than the first, loose.

One hour later, they hit the main trail

which wound through the country towards Twin Buttes. Another two hours' ride should see them in the town, thought Steve, and then they would know what Gruber had been doing during their absence. A mile along the trail and they would reach the Tennant ranch. Steve wondered if Sarah Tennant would be there. Somehow, the thought of the girl seemed to start a fire burning in his chest.

But when they turned the wide bend in the trail a little while later, to cut down into the rolling prairie, everything was driven with a shocking, terrible suddenness from his mind. He reined the sorrel sharply, sat in the saddle while the coldness passed through him, scarcely aware of the other men as they rode up to him and sat their horses, staring down into the valley, where the smoke was still curling up from the blackened ruins of the ranch. The walls were still standing, but the roof had crashed in when the flames had enveloped the building and smouldering beams hung lop-sided in the rooms now open to the sky.

'God in heaven,' said Doc Manston softly. The way he said it was something between a prayer and a curse. Steve urged his horse forward, down the slope, at a rapid trot, dropping from the saddle while the sorrel was still moving forward. Slowly, he made his way into the ruins, staring about him, resisting the urge to call her name. He knew, with a deep sickness inside him, that neither Sarah Tennant nor her father could still be alive in this. Either they had fled into the hills as soon as they had spotted the bunch of killers riding in, or they had remained behind to fight for their homestead as they had sworn they would do if Gruber ever rode against them to carry out his threat. Once he had learned that Steve and the posse were away chasing across the territory after the outlaw band, he had made his move. This was what Steve had heard during the night. This was the handiwork of those riders.

Methodically, scarcely aware of what he was doing, he searched among the ruins, looking for some sign that would tell him whether the girl and her father were still alive or whether they had been murdered by Gruber's men. But he found nothing. The fire had swept through the whole of the building. In the barn outside he found that several bales of straw had been piled high just inside the doorway, and fired with torches. Had he remained awake that time in the early morning, and looked in this direction, he must surely have seen the glow on the horizon from this holocaust.

At length, he turned and made his way back to where the rest of the men sat uneasy in their saddles. There was no talk as he swung himself up, gripping the reins in hands that were clawed, with fingers in which the knuckles stood out white under the skin from the nervous tension he was exerting. Sullen men rode along the trail leading into Twin Butte, men who rode under the leadership of a man who wore the star of the sheriff on his shirt and the hard, intense look of a man filled with a savage and burning hatred. His orders were given sharply and without explanation and the men obeyed them all without question. They had seen too much now, they knew what they were up against and what they were fighting for.

Every man in that posse had known and respected Tennant, knew him for a fair and honest man who sought to harm no one. They must have known Sarah since she had been a child. Now it was highly likely that they were dead, and certainly everything they had built, all that they had worked and struggled for, had been destroyed. The cattle had been moved from the grassy range Steve noticed as they rode the trail down through the green meadows, past the burnt-out hulk of the other ranch which had been burned down just a few days previous.

Stony-faced, Doc Manston rode beside him, not speaking, not wishing to intrude upon the thoughts that were running through Steve's mind, knowing what the other was feeling at that moment.

The men who rode with him too, were hard-faced, tight-lipped. They had thought, the previous day, when they had fought the outlaw band and emerged victorious, that they had fought their last battle and evil had been stamped out. Now they knew that this had only been the beginning, that they had only just begun to fight; and a lot more men would have to die before they had cleaned up the place so that decent men and women might live out their lives in peace and security. In the past, everything had happened to someone else, and these men had been content to leave it that way. So long as it did not touch them personally, they wanted no part of this fight, even though it must have been obvious to them all, that it was only a matter of time before Gruber's envious eyes were cast on their own ranches. Now, they were seeing the visible proof for themselves and Steve knew that it had shaken them to the core. These were changed men from those who had ridden out of Twin Buttes a couple of days earlier, hard men, filled with a determination to put a stop to this evil once and for all.

But Steve did not disillusion himself. He knew that even with these men, he stood little chance of defeating Gruber. With a hundred trained killers at his back, the other was in an unassailable position, unless all of the ranchers and their men, and the townsfolk, came out on his side.

'Don't take this too hard, Steve,' said Manston suddenly, breaking the uneasy silence which had laid on them for so long. 'This isn't your fault. We had to go out after those outlaws, otherwise the wagon trains would never have been safe to cross that stretch of desert. You couldn't have foreseen that Gruber would have done anything like this.'

'I ought to have known,' said Steve, with a trace of savage bitterness touching his tone. 'I should have realized that he would have taken this chance to attack the Tennant place. He's been threatening to do it for some time now. And I let those two go on thinking that everything would be all right, I even told Sarah that if I heard of anything in town which suggested that Gruber meant to ride out and attack them, I'd get to her before he did and warn them. Those riders must have taken them completely by surprise. They'd never have stood a chance of defending themselves.'

'They may still be alive,' said the other soberly. 'Don't give up all hope. We didn't find any bodies back there, did we?'

Steve swung in the saddle to face him. 'You figure that Gruber might have taken them alive?' There was a new hope in his tone.

Doc Manston shrugged. 'It's possible. He may have decided that, before you get too much of a menace, he would take a couple of hostages, thereby hoping to be able to force your hand. The trouble is, I reckon I know how you feel about Sarah. When it comes to choosing between love and duty, which is it to be? You won't have long in which to make up your mind.'

7

GUN THREAT

Steve's face was wooden as he rode at the head of the small posse into the main street of Twin Buttes. It was a town which several of the men with him had thought never to see again when they had come up against those outlaws far to the east. But here they were and there was still another job to do, a far bigger one than that which they had so recently accomplished successfully. Steve's eyes were alert as he rode slowly between the stores and saloons which fronted on to the street. Out of the corner of his vision, he saw several of the men, clustered around the largest of the saloons, in the distance, shade their eyes as they glanced along the street to make out the identity of the riders. Then the small group of men broke up and several pushed their way through the swing doors, vanishing into the saloon. Gone to warn Gruber that his plan had failed, that far from being dead, killed at the hands of the outlaws, Steve Yarborough and most of the men who had ridden out with him, were still alive and kicking, still as dangerous as before, if not more so. Perhaps they had seen the look on Steve's face, knew what it portended.

He reined his horse in front of the sheriff's office, slid to the ground, tethered it to the bar, then stamped inside the office. Doc Manston followed him and several of the men. The rest dispersed and made their way to their own homes. Seating himself in the chair at the back of the long desk, Steve forced his tired, beaten body to relax. Trouble was coming, he could sense it. Word would get around quickly that he was back in town. He could expect trouble from Gruber, but from the rest of the population, that was something he didn't know. If his presence there, in defiance of the threat that Gruber had made against him, could show these people that it was possible to stand up to this vicious cattle baron who wanted to take everything from them, then at least, he had done something.

He did not have to wait long for trouble. There the sound of hurried steps outside on the boardwalk, and a moment later, the door of the office was thrown open and one of the barkeeps from the saloon across the street came in. He looked scared as he paused in front of the desk.

'Well?' Steve looked at him sharply. 'Did you want something?'

'Bart Gruber sent me,' quavered the other harshly. 'He's over at the saloon, asked me to step across and ask you to have a word with him over there. He says it's something important.'

Steve forced a grin. He sat up straight in the chair, pulled one of the Colts from its holster and laid it on the desk in front of him. He saw the look of fear in the barkeep's eyes and the sweat that popped out on his forehead. The other's hands twisted nervously with the apron around his middle.

'You'd better go back and tell Mister Gruber that as sheriff of this town, I give interviews here. I don't just step across to the saloon whenever he likes to give his orders. If he wants to see me about anything, I'm here. He knows where to find me. Tell him that.'

'I daren't. He'll kill me, Sheriff. He's–'

'Just tell him,' said Steve ominously. In his present mood, he did not feel like arguing, even with this man who was only carrying out orders, scared of what might happen to him. 'Now get over there, pronto.'

The other stared down at the gun on the desk for a long hesitant moment, then ran the tip of his tongue around dry lips, turned on his heel and went out of the door. Steve could hear his shuffling footsteps on the boardwalk for an instant, before the other stepped down into the dust of the street. He turned to Doc Manston. 'If you're right about Gruber holding those two as hostages, we've got little choice when it comes to hard bargaining, have we?'

'Not much,' agreed the other reluctantly. 'All you can do is try to bluff your way with him. You did right in asking him to come over here. In the saloon, there are too many places where he could have one of his men hidden, ready to shoot you in the back the minute he gave the signal.'

'You think that he'll come over here?' Steve lifted his brows into an interrogative line.

'I think he will. He's anxious to make sure that you do nothing more against him; and he figures that the only way for him to do that is to get in his threat of reprisal first. He knows that with the girl and her father in his hands, he holds a pretty good hand.'

Steve nodded. He sat quite still in the chair, outwardly relaxed; but inside, a host of thoughts and half-formed ideas were racing chaotically through his mind, questions to which he could not formulate any answers; and all the while, there was the feeling, overriding everything else in his mind, that time was running out fast for him. Whatever happened, he must not allow this man to harm Sarah Tennant or her father. Their lives were in his hands, and the realization and the responsibility weighed heavily on him. He glanced up at a sudden sound outside and a moment later, Bart Gruber stood framed in the doorway.

There was a pleasant smile on the other's face and he walked into the room quite openly. He wore guns, low on his waist, but he made no move towards them.

'I understand that you wanted to see me,' said Steve evenly. He motioned to the empty chair in front of the desk. 'What can I do for you, Gruber?'

The other shrugged. The smile was still there but there was a hint of glacial menace at the back of his eyes, eyes which did not stray from Steve's face for a single moment. He leaned back, outwardly as relaxed as Steve tried to appear.

'I hear that you managed to round up that outlaw gang operating in the desert way out to the east of here,' said the other. 'That was quite a feat. I would never have thought the posse would have gone through with it. Seems that they've got a new reserve of strength that I hadn't suspected before.'

'It certainly looks that way,' acknowledged Steve, wondering where this line of talk was leading. 'Trouble is that we found one of your men with them. We spotted him riding in that direction and figured that he might have been sent by someone to warn the outlaws we were headed towards them. But we hit them before they were ready for us.'

Bart Gruber leaned forward in his chair, his elbows resting on the table in front of him, his eyes boring into Steve's. 'And this man who was with them – did you kill him too?'

'If you're afraid that he might testify against you, Gruber,' said Doc Manston harshly, 'then you're lucky. He's dead, together with all of that renegade band. We're well rid of them, but we have enough evidence to prove that they were working hand in glove with you.'

'I'm afraid that I don't know what you're talking about,' said the other easily. 'Just because one of my men rides out to meet these outlaws, is no proof that I have had anything to do with them. I don't question where all of my men go when they're through working for me. If they want to ride out to these outlaws, then I can't stop them.'

'No, of course not.' There was open disbelief in the doctor's voice. He stared hard at Gruber. 'But you must admit that it looks mighty strange him riding out there to warn them we were on their trail. He wouldn't risk his life like that unless he'd been ordered to go.'

Gruber turned his keen-eyed gaze back to Steve. 'I think you'd better warn the doctor of the seriousness of the charges he's making, Sheriff,' he said calmly. 'You're supposed to be the law around here. Then you'd better enforce it.'

'That's just what I aim to do,' said Steve tightly. 'But first, I'd like to know what you know about the attack on the Tennant ranch during the early hours of this morning.'

Gruber's lips went back in a faintly mocking smile. 'I had heard about that,' he admitted. 'A tragic affair. But I had always warned them there were outlaws in the area. They refused to take heed of my warnings. Now it's happened as I prophesied it would and they've only themselves to blame.'

Steve shook his head slowly. There was a

hard edge to his voice. 'As I remember it, Gruber, you didn't prophesy that, you made it as a direct threat against the Tennants. Seems you have a very convenient memory for things like that. There's no doubt in my mind it was your men who carried out that attack. Whether or not you were there in person, doesn't make the slightest bit of difference. If you gave the orders, then you're legally and morally responsible.'

There was a sudden cold fury in the other's face. White and angry, he forced himself to his feet and stood there, glaring down at Steve with snapping eyes. 'You're making a big mistake,' he said thinly, through tightly clenched teeth. 'But I warned you too of what might happen if you persisted in running the law in this town. All right, so you want all of our cards on the table. Perhaps that would be best for everyone concerned. I'll admit that it was my men who rode out on the Tennant ranch and burned it to the ground. Both the girl and her father are still alive and as well as can be expected. But how long they stay that way depends on you.'

Steve remained silent, knowing what was coming next. 'I see you got my meaning, Yarborough. Your days as sheriff here are finished as of now. If you aren't out of Twin Buttes by sundown, both the girl and her father will be strung up from the nearest tree and I'll have all of my men out looking for you, with orders to gun you down on sight. You may be able to kill one or two of them, but the odds are a hundred to one against you living through the night. You can't kill all of them, that much must be obvious, even to you. Just think it over, Sheriff.' He deliberately stressed the last word sneeringly as he walked back towards the door. In the opening, he paused: 'I wouldn't advise you to try to find either of them. It'll be the simplest thing in the world for my men to kill them, before you could ever get to them.'

White-faced, Steve watched him go and felt the heaviness of defeat settle over him as he sank back into the chair. Gruber was right, of course. There did seem to be nothing he could do and he knew, instinctively, that the other would carry out his threat.

'What are you going to do?' asked Manston quietly. He came forward and stood in front of the desk. There were deep lines scored beneath his eyes and a weariness that showed through into his voice. But he still held himself tautly upright as he went on:

'Whatever it is, we'll understand and back you to the limit. Everyone knows Gruber for what he is now.'

'Mebbe so. But I can't let him carry out that threat to kill Sarah Tennant and her father,' protested Steve tightly.

'But how do you know that they're still alive? You've only got his word for it. And even if they are, you can't be sure that he'll keep his word to let them go, even if you do ride out of town.'

That made sense, Steve told himself. Indecision was strong within him. It was hard for him to know what to do for the best. If he rode out of town it meant that all of the good he had done and for which four men had died, would be undone, and Gruber would be left in undisputed control of the town and the surrounding territory. If he stayed, and fought the other with everything at his disposal two innocent people would be killed out of hand.

He pulled himself together sharply. 'Is there anyone in town who might know where he's keeping them?' he asked harshly. 'If not, do you reckon we could get hold of one of his men, force him to tell us while there's still time?'

Manston rubbed one hand over his

stubbled chin. 'It isn't likely that many of his men would know,' he said soberly. 'Gruber is a clever man. He'll have foreseen that move on your part.'

'Perhaps.' Steve got swiftly to his feet, picked up his gun from the table, checked it, then thrust it back into its holster. 'But it's the only chance we've got.'

'I agree. But it's not the kind of chance I'd like to risk two people's lives on. Besides, you have only until sundown. After that, it will be too late.'

'Then we'll have to move fast.' Steve moved to the door. 'I'm figuring on having until sundown without any trouble from Gruber. I reckon I know the kind of man he is now. He's trying to play with me like a cat with a mouse. He's so goddamned certain that I won't find 'em, that he won't bother trying to stop me.'

'But you can't do this alone, you'll need help,' protested the doctor. He looked at Steve with troubled eyes.

'No.' The other shook his dead decisively. 'I have to do this alone. But if I don't get back by sundown, I want you to get the men together and move in against Gruber. They may follow you now.'

'You're a fool if you reckon that you can

find where he's got them hidden all by yourself,' protested the other. 'At least, let one of us come with you.'

Steve gave a further quick shake of his head. 'Gruber will be expecting something like that and he'll have men watching every trail out of town. One man might be able to slip through whereas any more could be easily spotted. I stand a far better chance this way.'

'You reckon he's got them holed up some place out of town?' There was a faint note of surprise in the doctor's voice, tinged with a touch of bleak despair and defeat.

'I'm sure of it. In town, there are few places he could keep them hidden without someone knowing where they were. And he must know by now that he can trust only his own men, that the townsfolk are beginning to move against him. I figure that he'll have them some place to the south.'

'But that's empty country,' said the other quietly.

'I know. But he'll figure that's the last place we'd go to look for them. There are plenty of old abandoned mine workings out in that direction and they could be in any of a dozen of them. Places where they could be hidden out for days without being found.'

'He'll have men watching them. Nothing so sure as that.' The thin-faced man spoke up from the far corner of the room. 'If you won't let any of us come with you, at least I might be able to give you something you can turn to good account, just in case you want to pull off some of the guards.'

Steve watched him in surprise as he walked through the door at the back of the room. He was gone for less than five minutes. When he came back, there was something in his hand which Steve recognized instantly. The other held out the slender, yellow sticks with the thin length of white fuse trailing from them.

'Dynamite.' Steve lowered his brows as he glanced at it, then took it gingerly in his hand. 'Where'd you get this?'

'Knew a couple of the engineers working on the railroad back east,' said the other quietly. 'Figured it might come in useful sometime. Reckon this is as good a time as any to use it. You know how to use it?'

Steve gave a quick nod. 'I'll find a way of using it to good advantage,' he promised. Turning on his heel, he went outside on to the boardwalk, fastened the dynamite carefully on to the saddle, aware of the eyes that watched him from further along the street in

215

the direction of the saloon. Gruber would be wanting to know every move he made, he thought grimly. Then he felt a tight sense of amusement rising inside him. But two could play at that game and he had thrown better men than these off his trail when he'd had a mind to, and now he was playing for high stakes. He could not afford to make a single mistake, could not allow the other to become too suspicious, otherwise both Sarah Tennant and her father would be as good as dead.

Swinging himself up into the saddle, he turned his sorrel and rode slowly along the street. There was a handful of horses tethered outside the hotel as he rode past and from the corner of his eye, he noticed the two grim-faced gunmen who came out and climbed into the saddle, turning their horses after him. At a steady pace, he rode out of town in the late morning heat, taking little notice of the men on his trail. A mile from Twin Buttes, he gave the sorrel its head, spurring it sharply. The powerful horse responded instantly, surging forward over the uneven ground. It could easily out-distance the others, Steve knew, but for the moment, he wanted the men trailing him to keep him in sight. He did not want them to lose him too soon, or they might guess that he had switched trails and was heading back towards town. Ahead of him lay rocky, scrub-covered country. Swiftly, he put the horse along the narrow trail that wound up into the rocks. Down below, the pursuing men did likewise, gigging their mounts in order to keep him in sight.

Here, no trail would show in the hard ground. Pulling the sorrel around with a swiftness that would have unseated any lesser rider, he plunged down into a narrow canyon cut in the rock, moved into shadow, halting the horse, holding his hand over its nostrils. There was the steady thunder of hoofbeats as the men on his trail thundered after him. They did not pause as they came alongside his hiding place. Driving their mounts to the punishing limit, they swept on along the trail, the sound of hoofs fading swiftly into the distance. Satisfied, Steve turned his mount, came out on to the trail once more and rode quickly back along the way he had come.

He expected no further trouble from either of those two men. But the most difficult part of the task he had set himself, still lay in front of him. A quarter of a mile from the outskirts of the town, he slid from the saddle, tethered the sorrel to a handy

217

cottonwood and made his way into Twin Buttes on foot. Deliberately skirting the main street, knowing that although Gruber's men would have relaxed their vigilance temporarily after he had ridden out of town, there was still danger there, he moved towards the rear of the saloon. If there was one person in Twin Buttes who could tell him where Gruber had taken Sarah Tennant and her father, it was the woman who called herself Babette Laredo, perhaps the real driving force behind Gruber.

Gruber had evidently been so sure that his two hired killers could trail Steve and follow him all the way clear of town, reporting back on his movements, that there was no guard at the rear of the saloon. Steve studied the back of it for several minutes, feeling the silence of the noonday heat close around him. The guns lay heavy against his thighs and he had taken the precaution of bringing the long lariat with him from his horse's saddle. Just as he had figured, it would be possible to climb up the back of the long building on to the balcony which ran its entire length.

He smiled grimly to himself as he edged cautiously forward along the backs of the buildings. Once, a man's hoarse voice reached him from somewhere close at hand and he froze into the shadows, one hand on the butt of his gun, ready to jerk it from its holster if the other showed himself. But after a few moments, there was silence again. By now, Gruber would be relaxed and unworried, believing him to be a long way away, on a wild goose chase, having probably ridden out of town in the wrong direction. There was a back door to the saloon, and a couple of windows on either side of it, with their shutters drawn against the glaring sunlight. For a moment, he debated whether simply to burst inside, rely on his gun to deal with any trouble he might run into, then he decided against such a move. Stealth was still needed here. Going in like that would lean too much towards a luck which might not be with him.

The lariat made only a faint whisper of sound as it spun high in the air, the noose settling smoothly over the upjutting post at the end of the balcony. He pulled it tight with a gentle jerk, tested it once, then put all of his weight on it, pulling himself up slowly, hand over hand. There was a risk here, too, but it was nothing compared with going into that saloon through either of the doors. Five minutes later, he swung himself silently, catlike, on to the balcony. Behind one of the windows which opened out on to it, he would find Babette Laredo and he knew with a sharp sense of grim determination that if she knew anything of the whereabouts of Sarah Tennant and her father, she would talk. He was in no mood for being gentle with anyone. Gruber's hold on this place had to be smashed, utterly and completely. The tinkling melody from a tinny piano sounded from the room below as he edged slowly along the balcony, listening at every window. Behind most of them lay silence. Then, outside the window nearest the far end, he paused, holding himself motionless as the sound of voices reached him. They were the voices of two women and he recognized one of them instantly as Babette Laredo.

Steve waited impatiently. He did not want to move in through that window to find two women there, possibly more. He wanted to get the woman alone, force her to say where the Tennants were being kept. After that, once he was well clear of the town and mounted, he would rely on the speed of his own horse to get him to the hideout before Babette could warn Gruber of what had happened. For a long minute, he stood out there on the balcony, in full view of any man who might come into that narrow street and stand sufficiently far from the boardwalk to glance up and see him. But the street slumbered in the hot noonday sun and he felt reasonably safe.

The women talked in low voices for what seemed an eternity. Then, inside the room, he heard the door close softly, followed by silence. Steve eased the gun from its holster, held it balanced in his right hand and opened the window quietly, stepping through into the room beyond. He had a brief glimpse of the tall, flame-haired woman in the dress which matched her hair, seated in front of the table before the mirror. She whirled instantly, eyeing him without a trace of fear on her face. Her brows shot up as she rose swiftly to her feet, glancing down at the gun in his hand.

'Just keep very quiet and you won't get hurt,' Steve said softly. He closed the window behind him and moved forward, further into the room.

'What is this?' she asked harshly. 'Have you gone insane, coming in here and holding me up with a gun? Who are you – and what do you want? Jewellery, money?'

'Keep quiet,' Steve deliberately made his

voice rough. 'I'll do the talking. I'm not here for fun. I want the answers to some questions, questions that I'm sure you can answer.'

'And what makes you think I will?' There was a note of defiance in her voice. She turned away from him and seated herself at the table, her hand going to one of the drawers. Before she could open it, Steve stepped forward swiftly, his left hand grasping her wrist. Very carefully, he opened the drawer, took out the small pistol which lay there and thrust it into his belt.

'That was very foolish,' he said harshly. 'Another move like that and you'll regret it.'

Her lips drew back in a sneering smile. 'Why – what will you do? Shoot me in cold blood. Even if you were a man who could do that, you wouldn't dare. One shot and you'll have Bart Gruber and his men swarming all over this place. You'd never get out of here alive.'

Steve raised his brows. 'That's true,' he conceded. 'But there are other means of silencing you or making you talk. I could draw the tip of the gunsight down your cheek and ruin that beautiful face of yours. Then Gruber might not find you quite so attractive and your position here wouldn't be worth a silver dollar.'

For the first time, he saw fear in the dark eyes and knew that what he had said, his threat, had struck home. 'That's better,' he said, as she crouched back in her chair. 'Now that you and I understand each other, perhaps you'll be a little more co-operative.' He moved forward and as he did so, the badge on his shirt showed through his open jacket. He saw her eyes widen as she realized who he was.

'You're Steve Yarborough, the man these fools made sheriff.'

'That's right.' He nodded slowly. 'I understand that Bart Gruber sent his men to raid one of the ranches last night. The ranch belonging to the Tennants. From what some of the men have told me, including Gruber himself, he has both Sarah Tennant and her father hidden away somewhere, with a handful of men guarding them. I think you know where they are, Babette. And you're going to tell me.'

'You fool.' She forced scorn into her voice. 'Even if I did know, what makes you think I'd tell you? Bart is the big man as far as this territory is concerned and nothing you or your few friends can do will stop him. You might as well give yourself up now and save a lot of trouble later.'

Steve was not impressed by her remarks, knowing that she was afraid deep down and trying desperately not to show it. His threat to disfigure her had struck deep, too deep, for her not to know that he had meant every word of it. For a long moment, she kept her eyes on the gun barrel that never wavered, only a few inches from her face.

'Don't try to bluff me, Babette.' Hardness edged his voice. 'You know where they are, all right. Now are you going to tell me or do I have to—' As he spoke, he thrust the barrel of the Colt forward until the tip of it touched her cheek, just below the right eye. She shrank back, tried to push herself deeper into the chair, but the cold metal followed her. Her lower lip began to tremble.

'Are you going to tell me where he's had them taken or do I have to force the truth out of you?'

'But Bart will kill me if he finds out that I've told you this and—' She broke off sharply at a sudden loud knock at the door. For a moment, Steve had the impression that she intended to risk a cry to the person on the other side of the door, then she saw the determination in his eyes and paused.

'Say that you're resting,' he said softly, his

voice little more than a hoarse whisper. 'Hurry!'

The woman swallowed, then called: 'Who is it?'

'It's me, Babette. Cora. Can I see you for a moment?'

'I'm resting, Cora.' A pause then, 'I'll come down in an hour or so.'

'Very well.' Steve listened carefully, heard the other's footsteps as she retreated along the passage outside. Then he turned to look down at the frightened woman in front of him.

'That's better,' he said quietly. 'Now are you going to tell me or do I have to mark you with the gunsight.' He moved the barrel forward a little, rested the tip of the sharp gunsight against the pale, smooth flesh of her cheek, saw her flinch and try to jerk her head back, to escape from the deadly touch of metal.

'All right, damn you, I'll tell you.' She almost hissed the words at him, her lips drawn back over her teeth. 'But I hope to God that Bart catches up with you. I want to be there when he kills you. I want to see you die!'

'I wouldn't be too sure of that,' snapped Steve impatiently. 'Now, where are they being kept, and no tricks mind. If you give me the wrong steer, I'll come back and make sure the next time.'

'He's had them taken to the old Carver place. It's five miles south of here near the old mine workings. They haven't been harmed yet, but he means to kill them if you don't do as he says and get out of town before sundown.'

'Thanks.' Steve moved a couple of feet to the rear, holding the gun on her. 'And how many men has he got out there watching them?'

'I don't know.' Her voice quavered a little. 'I swear before God that I don't know. You've got to believe that.'

It was obvious from her face that she was speaking the truth on that point. No matter, Steve reflected, it was something he would have to discover for himself. He eyed the woman closely. He could not run the risk of having her going straight down the stairs outside and spilling all of this to Gruber. He needed a head start if he was to get both the girl and her father out of Gruber's hands. Glancing about him, he caught sight of the long, silken handkerchief on the table. Swiftly, he picked it up, twisted it in his hands until it formed a strong cord, then made the other turn around while he tied her hands and ankles together. Another handkerchief as a gag and he lifted her in his arms, carried her to the wide, airy cupboard on the far side of the room and placed her in it, closing the door. The girl named Cora would undoubtedly come back in an hour's time and, getting no reply to her knocking, would come in and find her.

Swiftly, he pouched the gun, went back to the window and stepped out on to the balcony. As he started to move forward, he heard the door below him open. Freezing into immobility, he stood there, holding his breath, listening to the man's gruff voice which sounded almost immediately below him. The slurred speech told him that the other was drunk and there was a better than even chance that he would not see the lariat which still dangled over the balcony on to the street below. Setting his teeth, he waited. There came a few staggering steps, then the man was out in the middle of the narrow, dusty street, walking slowly away from the saloon, his head lolling forward on his chest, eyes staring at the ground beneath his feet as he walked.

Steve exhaled slowly. The other had not seen the rope. That much was certain. His luck had held. Swiftly, he climbed down it, reached the street just as the other man, his back still towards him, turned the far corner into the main street. Cautiously, Steve made his way between dingy, tumble-down houses which stood in the hot, shimmering heat, their slanted roofs almost touching the ground.

Then he was outside the town, walking swiftly to where he had left his sorrel tethered. There was no sign of the men who had trailed him into the hills as he swung up into the saddle, and no indication of any pursuit from the direction of the town. Turning the sorrel's head, he moved to the south. There was little time to waste. A few short hours to sundown, and whatever happened, he had to have the Tennants out of Gruber's hands by that time. He knew that Doc Manston would do everything in his power to keep his word and lead as many of the ranchers and townsfolk as he could muster against Gruber. But Steve doubted if that would be enough. Those men would fight, but only half-heartedly, until they knew that old Clancy Tennant and his daughter were safe. Then they would see for themselves that Gruber wasn't as all-powerful as he had tried to appear, and that knowledge ought to prove the turning point in this battle against tyranny.

The sun climbed up to the zenith as he left the lush green belt of the cattle country behind and headed into the unwelcome lands which lay due south of Twin Buttes. Gradually, the terrain changed. It grew more inhospitable and treacherous. There were few recognizable trails here. Most of them had been obliterated by storms and landslides since the old mines had been worked out and no one ever came here now, except for a small handful of gold prospectors still following a dream, and outlaws such as those men of Gruber's.

At a steady pace, he rode over the rough ground, cutting into the rocky country, skirting wide chasms which, in places, plunged straight down for a sheer hundred feet on either side of the trail. Around him, the ground seemed to have been carved out into knife-edged areas of sun and shadow.

It was not until he had been riding for the best part of an hour, with the noonday heat heavy and clinging around him, that he spotted the tracks of several horses in the soft mud around a waterhole among the rocks. The tracks undoubtedly fresh, had been made less than two days previously and the sudden conviction came to him that Babette had spoken the truth and he was on the right trail.

He stopped the horse for ten minutes and let it blow. Ahead, lay some of the most difficult country in the whole territory. It was senseless to push the sorrel to its limit. He might need its strength and speed when he had to head back to town. He began to feel a little easier in his mind as he gigged the horse on again, sitting high in the saddle, shading his eyes occasionally against the sun, ready to pick out the first sign of the outlaws ahead of him. The thought of the dynamite packed in the saddle-bag gave him a feeling of power. By now, the sun was at its zenith, a white-hot finger laid on his back and shoulders. It was a terrible trail, but there was the consolation that it was highly probable that when they had taken their two captives along it, it had been night time, the air would have been considerably cooler than this. He watched constantly ahead, each side, and occasionally behind him, back in the direction he had come, because it was from that direction that pursuit would come once Gruber discovered that he had forced the truth out of Babette. Gruber would waste no time in following him, knowing that once he got Sarah and her father away from that place, his own life would be in deadly danger.

In places, the trail was almost completely obliterated and then again, it would suddenly become clear again as it angled high up the side of the redstone canyons, around steep bends which skirted the meandering sandstone walls of the bluffs. By the time he had travelled for another hour and every nerve and fibre in him screamed with the agony of heat, and his flesh seemed to have been seared by red-hot knives, where the dust had laid its itching, irritating fingers on him, he reached the end of the bluffs and paused, looking down into the low hills, where the mine workings began. He scanned the empty desolation which lay in front of him, eyes narrowed, then paused as he spotted the tiny cabin which stood on the edge of the mining area. That was obviously the place, he decided. The sight sent a little thrill through him. From now on, he would have to exercise caution. They might have men watching the trails, just on the off chance that he had somehow managed to find them. After what had happened to the outlaw band in the desert, it was doubtful if Gruber would take any more chances like that. He put the horse to the trail, rode down into the wide valley floor. There was plenty of cover here, the ground being broken up by tall rocks which rose out of the valley floor, and narrow canyons which speared through them.

There was no sound around him as he neared the old Carver home, apart from the faint cries of the buzzards which wheeled endlessly overhead, like tattered strips of black cloth against the heavens. The sight of them sent a little shiver through him and he tightened his lips into a hard line. A few hundred yards from the homestead, he dismounted and tethered the horse to an old tree stump which thrust itself from the hard, arid ground like some fossil of a bygone age.

The sun beat down upon him, almost blinding him as he took the dynamite from the saddle-bag, checked that he had the box of long matches with him, then set off into the sunlit rocks, slitting his eyes against the glare. He walked in silence, speculating. Somehow, he had to get close enough to that place, to be able to use his gun, without giving any of the men there the chance to shoot the girl or her father. On the face of things, it seemed impossible. They would have had their orders to kill both of their captives rather than let him rescue them; and he knew enough of the men who worked for Gruber, to know with a sick certainty that they would carry out that order without pausing to think. There was no mercy in men like these. And above all, they would be afraid for their own skins, knowing that Gruber would shoot them down without question if they did not obey him.

His limbs and muscles ached with the tension of the long ride from the town, but he forced himself to move quickly, cat-like, through the rocks, keeping his head low as he approached the shack. There was no sound from that direction, but none of these men would be doing much talking, he reflected bitterly. Eyes alert, starting at every sudden sound or movement, he moved forward, moving laterally along the slope of the rock face. Then, turning around a large, nut-thrusting boulder, he saw the shack right in front of him with smoke curling from the chimney.

8

THE WAITING GUNS

Evidently the men inside the shack considered themselves to be safe from attack, otherwise they would never have lit that fire, giving away their presence there. Steve crawled forward until he lay on the very edge of the rocks, looking out across the intervening space towards the shack. It lay at least fifty yards away and every yard would mean that he would come under the guns of the men inside. Somehow, he had to discover how many there were there and find some way of getting them out and away from the girl and her father. Swiftly, he turned his head to look in every direction, then paused as his eyes took in the black, empty eye of the tunnel in the rock on the far side of the hut, which marked the position of the old mine workings in that area. Rusted rails still ran down into the black depths and a couple of old, broken wagons stood mellowing in the hot sunlight.

The minutes slipped by as he racked his brain for some plan which would give him a chance of success. As he lay there, the door of the shack opened and three men came out into the sunlight. They wore guns and stood for a moment, talking together. It was too far away for him to be able to make out any of the words, but after a moment, one of them went back into the shack while the others walked around to the rear. It was then that Steve noticed for the first time, the five horses tethered to a rope at the far side of the hut. His eyes narrowed as he picked them out. So that meant there were three of Gruber's men there, the other two horses having been used by Sarah and her father. At least, he knew what he was up against. Drawing a deep breath, he edged back into the rocks, as an idea began to form in his mind. Carefully, he examined the sticks of explosive which the thin-faced man had given him, checked the length of fuse, then nodded to himself, satisfied. Although he knew little of these things, he estimated that this length of fuse would burn for close on five minutes before the explosive went off. That should give him plenty of time to plant it and get back under cover, ready to move in to the attack.

Steve's hope now was for him to get at least two of those men sufficiently well away from the shack for him to be able to reach it and deal with the one man remaining. Once he had done that, he felt reasonably confident that he could deal with the other two when they discovered that they had been tricked and they came high-tailing it back to the homestead. Very carefully, keeping the rocks between him and the shack, Steve made his way deeper into the rocks, snaking along narrow defiles which caught his eye, all the time working his way around the wide clearing, in the direction of the ancient mine workings. He moved like a mountain cat in spite of the stiffness in his limbs but several times he was forced to stop for breath and once, the sensitive explosive jammed in a crevice in the rocks and he was forced to remain there for several precious minutes, easing it out, his heart in his mouth. He wasn't sure just how touchy this material was to impact and friction, but he wasn't going to take any chance on blowing himself up, after coming so far without incident. The knowledge that by now, Babette Laredo must have been discovered, bound and gagged in that cupboard, and that she had told everything she knew to Gruber, was a driving, intense thing at the back of his mind, forcing him on, urging him to do things twice as fast as he was doing them, even though caution and common sense told him that it could be fatal to hurry. Those men at the shack were not suspicious, not yet, but it needed only the slightest sound to bring them to the alert and then there could be hell to pay.

These men, too, had been able to rest up for a long time before he had caught up with them and they had not been forced to make that terrible ride in the full heat of the sun as he had. He hoped that this would not tell on him when time for action came. He came out of the rocks less than twenty yards from the mine entrance. Out of the corner of his eye, he could just make out the figures of the two gunmen, standing by the tethered horses. Evidently they were watering and feeding the animals, little guessing that danger and vengeance were so close. Steve had chosen this spot with care. It was at such a distance from the cave entrance, that he would be able to slip from the rocks and into the deep shadow without exposing himself to the others for more than a few seconds. There was still the risk that one of the men might see him, might glance up at the wrong moment, but that was a risk he would have to take.

Drawing a deep breath, he paused for a moment longer, then threw himself forward, out of the rocks and into the entrance, almost stumbling over the rusted metal rails which led into the interior of the mine. At any moment as he dived inside, he expected to hear the sudden crack of a Colt, to feel the shattering impact of a bullet striking into his back. But it never came. There was silence from the direction of the shack and he lay for a moment, with his shoulders against the rocky wall, breathing heavily, forcing his heart into a more normal beat.

Swiftly, he looked about him for a suitable place for the explosive, then spotted a ledge, at shoulder height, about twenty feet inside the opening. Carefully, he placed the explosive on it, packing it around with small stones and dirt, leaving only the end of the fuse showing. Going back to the entrance, he saw that the two men had gone back into the shack. Satisfied, he went back, struck one of the long matches and placed the flame against the end of the fuse. It caught instantly. There was a faint spluttering of flame as it began to burn along its snaking length. He paused for only a moment longer, then made his way quickly out of the tunnel, into the rocks again, working his way back along the way he had come until he was at the nearest point to the shack. Another three minutes at the most and that explosive would go off. What happened then, would be pure chance, but he was relying on the fact that none of these men had lived in this part of the territory long enough to know that no one had been among these mine workings for the best part of twenty years. Gruber may have told them that the seams had been worked out a long time before, but once they heard that explosion and saw the smoke and fumes pouring from the tunnel, he was hoping that they would think miners were still at work there and two of them would go out to investigate. It was unlikely that they would be ready to shoot down anyone they suspected of being there in cold blood. Gruber would have given them no orders concerning miners and prospectors; in fact he might even have warned them to arouse no suspicion with such men as they might meet on the trail. But these gunmen would want to make certain that there was no chance of anyone working the mine coming out and discovering them inside the shack. If he could panic two of the men into rushing into the mine, once they were sure it was safe to go in, then he stood a good chance of rescuing the girl and her father.

The minutes passed slowly. A tiny bead of sweat formed on his forehead and trickled down into his eyes. He blinked it away savagely, took out the guns from their holsters and held them ready in his hands. Every muscle and nerve in his body was tensed, waiting for that explosion. This plan had to work, he told himself fiercely. If it failed, then there was nothing else he could do. Frowning, he glanced up at the sun, then squinted in the direction of the tunnel mouth. Had that fuse failed? Surely it ought to have gone off by now. A hundred possibilities spilled through his mind as he lay there in the blistering heat of the sun, a hundred possibilities that were ended, shockingly, abruptly, as the thunderous explosion shattered the clinging silence, and he saw the billowing cloud of dense black smoke come pouring out of the tunnel entrance. A shower of stones and boulders crashed on to the trucks which stood outside on the rusted rails.

Scarcely had the rolling echoes died away

than the door of the shack burst open and the three gunslingers appeared in the opening. Two of them darted out and stared, open-mouthed, in the direction of the mine. The third said something in a harsh, urgent voice to them, gestured in the direction of the cloud of smoke that was now lifting into the clear air. The two men hesitated, then began to run in the direction of the mine, pulling the guns from their holsters as they ran. Dry-mouthed, Steve watched them go. Then reached the entrance to the tunnel and paused there, clearly debating whether or not it was safe to go inside, possibly considering that where there had been one explosion there could quite easily be another. Tensed like a coiled spring, he crouched there, waiting.

A moment later, one of the men caught the other by the sleeve and gestured him forward. They plunged into the slowly-settling smoke and vanished from sight. Without pausing, Steve hurled himself forward, gripping the heavy Colts tightly in his fists. He reached the door of the shack on the run, plunged inside, his guns coming up to cover the gunman who stood in the middle of the room, staring down at Sarah Tennant and her father, seated at the table in the middle of the single room.

'Hold it there – and not a sound,' said Steve harshly, There was some quality in his voice which halted the other. He wished that he could pull the trigger of his guns and kill the other out of hand, but such killing was not in him, was not part of his nature. Swiftly, reversing one of the guns, he brought the butt crashing down on the back of the man's skull. He pitched forward without a sound, crashing against the table, his knees buckling under him as he slid forward on to his face.

'Steve!' Sarah Tennant stared at him as though unable to believe her eyes. 'But Gruber told us that you had been killed by the outlaws when you rode out after them.'

'Then Gruber lied,' said Steve tightly. 'But quickly, there isn't a moment to lose.'

'There are two other men,' said Clancy Tennant harshly. 'They've gone–'

Steve nodded swiftly. 'I know. They've gone to see what that explosion was about. That was something I laid on for their benefit. But it won't take them long to find that out and they'll come high-tailing it back here. We've no chance of getting their horses and riding out. They could shoot us down before we got out of range. We'll have to finish them here, and quickly. By now, Gruber will know that I've come after you and there'll be a horde of his men on our tail.'

He went over to the window, stared out in the direction of the mine. The smoke had already dispersed and a moment later, the two men ran out, paused for an instant, then began to run in the direction of the shack.

'Here they come,' said Steve tightly. 'Let them get within range and then open fire. Shoot to kill.'

Clancy Tennant nodded in quick understanding. He had taken the guns from the man who lay unconscious on the floor. Now he stood close to one side of the window with Steve on the other. Outside, the two men came forward shouting. Evidently they were trying to warn their companion that something was wrong, thought Steve inwardly. He brought up his guns. Fifty yards and the men paused.

Some instinct, coupled with the fact that their companion had not come out in answer to their frantic shouting, must have warned them that this was a trap. But for them, it was too late. Even as they went down into a half crouch, Steve snapped: 'Right, Clancy. Give them everything you've got.'

He punctuated his own sentence with gunshots. The guns kicked in his hands again and again. The nearer of the two gunmen straightened up on his toes, arching his back into an unnatural posture as the bullets slammed home, boring holes in his chest, the stain on his shirt widening. There was shocked, frozen disbelief on his face as he pitched forward, knees giving way under him as though no longer able to take his weight. His body jerked and toppled and behind him, the second man, running forward, trying desperately to bring up the guns in his hands, loosed off a couple of shots that smashed into the woodwork of the shack, close to the window. But his aim had been hurried, thrown off by the speed with which things had happened. His hands clutched automatically at his chest, the gun falling from his fingers. He was dead before his body hit the ground.

Straightening up, Steve turned to the girl. 'It's finished out there,' he said tightly. 'But now we have to get out of here before any more of Gruber's sidewinders arrive on the scene. They can't be more than an hour behind me and they'll be driving their horses as fast as they can.'

'If we ride back to town, we'll run into

them,' said Clancy harshly. He thrust the guns into his empty holsters. 'You got anything figured out, Steve?'

'Not unless you know of another trail out of here. One that can take us back to Twin Buttes before nightfall.'

'There is another trail, over the mountains,' admitted the other softly. 'But it won't be easy to get back by nightfall. Why so particular about that?'

'It's too long a story to explain right now.' Steve went to the door and stared out into the sunlit rocks. 'But Gruber gave me until nightfall to ride out of Twin Buttes, otherwise he was going to see that both of you were killed. In answer to that, I decided to come out and look for you myself, but I gave Doc Manston orders to get as many of the townsfolk and ranchers together as he could and ride against Gruber by nightfall, if I didn't make it back by then. He'll do that, but I reckon there'll be few men who'll fight Gruber unless they have living proof that he can be beaten. If I can get back there with you, then I guess that'll give them all the encouragement they need.'

'Then we've got to make it,' said Sarah Tennant decisively. 'Even if we have to go over the mountains.'

'She's right.' Clancy nodded. 'But I reckon you'd better take one of the horses tethered at the back of the homestead. They'll be a mite fresher than yours and we'll need every ounce of speed and stamina we can get out of them if we're to make it back to Twin Buttes in time.'

'Do you think Gruber will come out here with his men to look for you?' asked the girl as they saddled the horses, then mounted.

Steve shook his head. 'That ain't likely,' he answered. 'He'll want to be back there in Twin Buttes, to see if I still show my face in town by sundown. He knows that the showdown will come tonight and he's determined to be there when it happens.'

'Makes sense, I suppose,' agreed the older man. He touched spurs to the horse and led the way into the rocks past the mine working and in the opposite direction to that along which Steve had come. He brought up the rear, following the girl. Things were going to be neatly cut, he reflected tightly. It was possible, as the buzzards flew, this was a shorter route into Twin Buttes, but it was a terrible trail which led over these mountains; he doubted if it was one which had been used by anyone other than mountain cats and Indians.

Slowly, they wound their way along the mountain trail. The sun, even though it had dipped slightly past its zenith, still blazed down upon them, dancing off the rocks in waves of shocking, dizzying heat. He felt sick and stunned by it and time and time again, his head jerked forward on to his chest, his eyes lidding and closing with weariness that threatened to close over him in a numbing wave. The trail narrowed in places so that it was impossible for two of them to ride side by side and they were forced to move in single file as the horses picked their way slowly forward over loose shale and rocks, the first wrong move being enough to send them crashing down into the deep gullies which opened up on either side of them.

Again and again, his mind told him that they were making too slow progress, that at this rate, it would be impossible for them ever to reach the town in time. And he knew that Doc Manston would stand little chance against Gruber's hired killers and gun-slingers with the few men behind him, who would really back him up, men who had the foresight to know that a showdown had to come, even if it meant that some good men would die.

Everything now seemed to depend on him reaching Twin Buttes in time. He wanted to call out to Clancy Tennant to move more quickly, then suppressed the urge. The other knew this route, knew what he was doing. To force the horses beyond this speed would mean asking for trouble. Perhaps, a little further on the trail would improve and they would be able to move more quickly.

But instead, the trail, if anything, was worse. They reached several spots where it seemed to be literally impassable and he was forced to sit impatiently in the saddle while Clancy went forward slowly, pausing to check the treacherous ground over which they had to pass. They were now high in the mountains which bordered the southern end of the grasslands and already the sun was beginning to dip swiftly towards the south-western horizon, bringing the long shadows which made things more difficult than before. Their horses tired with the effort. In this terrible country, only goats and mountain cats could live.

'How much further do we have to go, Clancy?' Steve called, as the other reined his horse for what seemed the hundredth time to examine the trail ahead.

'Another five miles or so,' called the other. 'We ought to be moving down into the prairie soon though, then we'll make better time.'

Steve sucked in a sharp breath, nodded helplessly. He was in the other's hands now. Any thought that he could ride on ahead of them, he dismissed at once. But there was no trace of worry on the older man's face. It was as if he were certain that they would make it. The minutes lengthened into an hour. The sun was a ball of red fire moving down the sky, throwing the long, black shadows over the rocks and crags. Then, almost before he was aware of it, they were no longer ascending. The trail was dipping downwards, widening in places as they crossed the peak and began to cut down the far side. The going became easier but it was still dangerous to hurry too much.

Most of the dragging fatigue had been washed out of Steve's body now, with the knowledge of what lay ahead of him once they reached Twin Buttes. It was possible that Gruber knew of this trail also and just to take no unnecessary chances he had dispatched some of his men to watch it, men ready to shoot as soon as they showed up. But somehow, Steve doubted that. Gruber would give them a little credit for common sense and no one in their right mind would ride over the mountains, especially with a girl and an old man. Besides, Gruber needed every man he could spare in the streets of Twin Buttes that night. He would send only those few necessary to follow his trail out to the old Carver place.

Half an hour later, they rode down out of the mountains and into the cattle country. Even though his mount was dead beat after that terrible ride over the mountain trail, Steve did not spare it now, but dug his spurs into its flanks, urging it forward. The sun was close to the western horizon now where clouds were stretched like a wall of flame across the sky. Clancy Tennant and Sarah kept up with him, although it was clear that they had almost reached the limit of their endurance. It would have been so easy to ease up now that they had hit the good country, but Steve knew that to do so would possibly mean that far more men would be killed out there in the streets of Twin Buttes than necessary. He had a responsibility towards these men too, one which he meant to honour with all the means in his power.

They reached Twin Buttes just before sundown. The town was quiet in front of them as they rode into the main street. No one was in sight and for a moment, it reminded Steve of the old ghost towns he had seen so often, stretched over the face of the country, as the tide of civilization had pushed itself steadily westward over the years. But this town was not empty and it had a strange and terrible waiting quality hanging over it that sent a little shiver coursing through his body. He sat tall and straight in the saddle, eyes probing the dimness of the night as he rode slowly forward.

It was not until he came within sight of Doc Manston's place that he noticed the horses outside and the silence took on a new meaning for him. Even as he rode up, the door opened and Manston's voice called: 'That you, Steve?' There was both surprise and disbelief in the other's voice.

Steve reined his horse, slid from the saddle. 'Yeah it's me,' he called. 'What's happening around here? Where's Gruber?'

'He's holed up in the saloon at the other end of the street. He's been bringing in men all afternoon. A small handful of them rode out of town just after noon, heading south. Reckoned they were hot on your trail and–' The other paused as Sarah Tennant and her father came forward.

'Well, I'll be–You managed to find them.' There was exultation in the other's voice.

'Sure.' Steve nodded, then became business-like. 'How many men have you?'

'Forty-seven,' answered the other. 'I'd hoped for more, but most of the ranchers didn't want to risk their lives and homesteads just because you said Gruber could be beaten. They may join us, but I doubt it. The same goes for most of the townsfolk. They've got off the streets and barricaded themselves in. They want no part of this either.'

Steve tightened his lips. Forty-seven men, forty-nine including Clancy Tennant and himself. They wouldn't stand too much of a chance against the hundred or so men that Gruber could muster up, men who lived by killing and destroying, men who had prices on their heads in half a dozen states and knew that they would have nothing to lose by dying. How much chance had they now?

He saw the look of bleakness in the other's eyes and had his answer there. But they had to go through with it now. They had no other choice. His keen eyes swept the men assembled there, taking in the grim, tight faces that peered back at him in the light of the lamp on the desk. He licked his lips thinly and stepped forward, aware of their eyes on him, knowing that they were looking to him for leadership and reassurance.

'You all know why we're here,' he said hoarsely, 'To put an end to Gruber and his dreams of power. There has to be a showdown, otherwise he'll continue to destroy each of you in turn. Together, we can stand against him and finish him for good. If we don't, then one by one, he'll destroy you. You all know what he has done in the past. If you want further proof, I'm certain that Sarah Tennant and her father can give it to you. But there's very little time for that. You all heard what Doc said. Gruber is holed up in the saloon along the street. It's pretty clear to me that he isn't quite as sure of himself even now as he would like us to think, otherwise he would have been here by now, attacking us instead of waiting for us to attack him.'

'You figuring on going out there and attacking him, Sheriff?' asked one of the men quietly. If there was any fear in the man's voice, Steve could not detect it.

He nodded. 'That's the best strategy in this case. We'll attack him before he's ready for us. It may have the result of bringing a few more of the townsfolk in on our side. If they see that we mean business, it may sway them to join us. If not, then we'll go down fighting. Every one of you, whether he knows it or not, has something to fight for. Freedom to live your lives as you like, without having to knuckle down to men like Gruber. Freedom to herd your cattle and get the best price you can for them, without having to live in continual fear of having them rustled from under your very noses, or having your ranches burned down about your ears as has happened to so many of the smaller ranches in these parts. We've got to make up our minds that we're going to end this, once and for all.'

'But he already outnumbers us by two-to-one,' said another man, watching Steve steadily. 'What chance do we have against those odds?'

'Pretty good, if we stick together,' said Steve. 'Which of you men are with me in this? I want nobody with me who's afraid to go through with it.'

None of them demurred and he led the way towards the door, paused as he found Sarah Tennant beside him, a rifle in her hands, a look of grim determination on her face.

He shook his head. 'This is no place for

you. Sarah,' he said softly. 'I want you to stay here, help with any of the wounded.'

The girl held her head high and there was an expression of defiance in her eyes. 'My place is out there with you,' she said harshly. 'I can use a rifle as good as any man and I have a score to settle with Gruber just like the rest of you. Besides, you'll need every gun you can get.'

'No,' said Steve firmly. 'Do you think I would be able to fight there, knowing that you were around, that you might be hit? I said you'll stay here and that's final.' For a moment, he thought that she still intended to defy him, then with a sudden shrug of her shoulders, she stepped back and laid the rifle back in the rack near the door. She did not lift her eyes to look at him as he moved away with the others, out into the empty, seemingly deserted street.

Slowly, in a band, they made their way along the street in the direction of the saloon. Steve noticed as they approached there were few lights in the windows. Evidently Gruber and his men did not intend to make good targets of themselves.

Fifty feet from the saloon, Steve paused, moved ahead of the others. In a loud voice, he called: 'You in there, Gruber. Better tell your men to give themselves up. We mean business this time.'

A pause, then Gruber's voice reached him from one of the windows. 'You still around, Yarborough? I seem to recall that I gave you until sundown to get out of town. Seems you can't take a friendly warning.'

'You're finished, Gruber,' snapped Steve harshly. 'And as for the Tennants, Clancy is here with us and his daughter is safe, where you'll never get her.'

There was silence for a long moment, then the sudden bark of a rifle sent Steve plunging swiftly to one side. The slug whined harmlessly through the air where his head had been a moment earlier.

'I'm warning every man who's with you, Yarborough, either throw down their guns and get back to their homes or I'll personally see to it that they're finished here.'

A hail of gunfire from the windows of the saloon rang out and the men in the street scattered to both sides, firing as they went down under cover. There came the sound of shattering glass as several of their bullets struck home. The crash of gunfire rolled back and forth along the street. Bullets struck the hard dirt and ricocheted in all directions. Further along, the horses tethered outside the surgery stomped their feet in fright as the sound rose to a savage crescendo.

Crouched down behind a barrel on the boardwalk, Steve fired shot after shot at the fleeting shadowy figures that showed themselves for brief moments at the windows of the saloon. He saw several of them fall back with loud cries as his sixguns tore home into their bodies. But it was soon obvious that with so many men at his back, Gruber held the whip hand.

Beside him, Clancy Tennant hissed sharply: 'They're sending out some of their men, Steve, over there at the corner.'

Steve turned his head sharply, peering into the dimness of the night. He caught the movement instantly, as a handful of men slipped out of the side entrance to the saloon, moved a little way along the street, into a position from where they could fire on the men already under cover and protected from the guns in the saloon itself.

'Give me some covering fire,' he whispered hoarsely, turning to the other. He slithered away along the boardwalk, ignoring the bullets that whined around his body. There was a desperate urgency within him now that drove him on to the exclusion of everything else. Another volley crashed out from the men crouched down further along the street, and he was forced to pull his head down and lie there for a long moment, while slugs hummed viciously like a crowd of angry hornets over his body, pinning him down, unable to move without committing virtual suicide.

Gradually, the firing slackened. Twisting, he pushed himself up on his elbows and wormed his way forward. More window glass smashed in the saloon as the men behind him continued to fire. Reaching the end of the boardwalk, he slithered down into the street, pushed himself swiftly to his feet and in a single motion, hurled himself under cover, into a position where he could bring his own fire to bear on the men less than twenty feet away. They had already seen the danger, were trying to bring their own guns to bear on him, but Clancy Tennant's fire was keeping them pinned down and now the tables were turned with a vengeance.

Swiftly, keeping his head down, he crammed fresh shells into the chambers of his guns, then opened up on the men close by. Two fell sideways as his slugs caught them in the chest, The others hesitated for a moment, then got to their feet and in blind fear, tried to run back under cover. Exposing themselves to Tennant's fire, none of them made it. Less than a minute later, they were all dead in the middle of the street and that particular menace had been removed.

Swiftly, Steve worked his way back to the others. Several of the men had been hit and had gone back to the surgery where Sarah was waiting to tend their wounds. In spite of the terrible hail of fire which had been poured into the saloon, there was no doubt in Steve's mind that Gruber still held the upper hand. He could guess at the other's plan, why he had been content to stay there and wait for Steve and the others to come to him. He was merely biding his time, keeping his men under cover, waiting until a high proportion of the ranchers and townsfolk had been wounded or killed, were low in ammunition, then he and his men would sally out of the saloon and overwhelm the survivors by sheer weight of numbers.

These suspicions were justified less than ten minutes later. The fire from the men crouched down on either side of the street had dwindled appreciably over the past few minutes. Gruber evidently judged that the time was right for him to make his own play.

A crashing volley of gunfire from the saloon which forced Steve and the others to duck hastily under cover; and then the gunmen from the saloon came pouring out into the street, firing from the hip as they came.

The men on the far side of the street began to fall back in confusion as the bullets struck among them. Desperately Steve pumped shot after shot into the crowd of men who advanced upon them, knowing with a sick certainty that he would not be able to hold them, that his own men were close to panic and that Gruber had won.

'Fall back to the surgery,' he yelled harshly at the top of his voice, to make himself heard above the crashing din of gunfire. 'It's the only chance we've got.' There was no sense in the men staying there to be killed. Brave as they were, it would be a senseless way in which to die.

Defeat lay heavy within him as he moved back along the boardwalk, firing as he did so. He saw two of the gunmen stumble and go down as his bullets found their mark. By now, most of Gruber's men were out in the open and he could just make out Gruber himself, well in the background, urging his men forward.

So they had fought and lost and now

Gruber was still in control and– There was a sudden commotion behind him, a sound which he had heard before, but which he had never expected to hear at that moment. Swiftly, he turned, stared in wild disbelief as the surging horde of mounted men rode headlong down the street, firing as they came, urging on their horses with wild cries. He knew then, in that moment, that the ranchers had not let him down, that they had backed him in time.

For a moment, the gunmen held their ground. Then, without waiting for any order from Gruber, they turned and fled, trying to get back to the saloon from which they had just come. But against the horsemen they stood no chance. Steve moved forward swiftly as the mounted ranchers and their men ran the gunmen down. The battle was short and decisive. Those who had not been shot down, threw their arms into the air as the grim-faced men from the ranches spread around Twin Buttes dismounted in front of the saloon.

Hurrying forward, eyes alert, Steve tried to pick out the tall figure of Bart Gruber whom he had noticed a few moments earlier. It was unlikely that the other would surrender, knowing only too well what was in store for him at the hands of the citizens of the town. And he would have made certain that, in the event of things going against him, he would have a means of getting away. Turning the corner at the side of the saloon, he caught a glimpse of the cattle baron leaping into the saddle of the waiting horse. Swiftly, he brought up the gun, fired instinctively at the other. The bullet missed as the other pulled around the horse's head and rode it straight for him. There was no mistaking the other's intention. He recognized the fact that he had been defeated, that the empire he had built up over the years of fear and murder had crashed down about his ears. But he still intended to escape and seeing the man who had been instrumental in accomplishing this in front of him, he was determined to ride him down. There was barely time for Steve to fling himself to one side. His arm and shoulder crashed with a bone-shaking force against the wall as the horse scraped by him. Something struck him viciously on the side of the neck, forcing him to drop the gun. Out of his blurred vision, he saw Gruber ride into the main street, pull hard on the reins to bring the head of the horse around, urging him away from the men who were busy rounding up the gunmen who had followed him to death and capture.

Then, abruptly, over the hubbub of noise and shouting, Steve heard the sharp, unmistakable crack of a rifle. There was only the one shot, but it seemed to sear across his brain like a knife. He saw Gruber's horse rear up as the bullet struck it in the neck, ploughing through skin and striking the bone. For an instant, Gruber fought to retain his seat in the saddle. Then he pitched backwards with a wild, loud cry and fell to the ground. Steve started forward, then paused as the horse, mortally wounded, fell too, rolling on top of the body beneath it.

Weakly, Steve put out a hand for support and stood there, staring down at the crushed body of the man who had fought to take over this town and all of the surrounding territory, who had based his life, and his rule, on fear and death. Even though it seemed a just and fitting end to such a man, there was still a rising nausea in the pit of his stomach which he thrust down only with a conscious physical effort.

Slowly, he made his way out into the main street. The gunmen had all been disarmed and were being led away. In the saloon itself, the place was a complete shambles. Glass lay strewn all over the floor between the over-turned tables and several of the gunmen were dead where they had fallen. He turned as he saw Clancy Tennant and Doc Manston coming towards him. There was a streak of blood on Clancy's cheek, but the old, familiar grin was on his lips as he holstered his guns.

'We did it,' he declared proudly. 'We finished them just as we said we would.'

Steve nodded slowly. Gradually, a little of the warmth was coming back into his body. 'I reckon that's my work done here,' he said slowly. He glanced down at the star which glittered on his shirt. He fingered it absently for a moment. 'Reckon you'll be needing this back, Doc, now that Gruber is finished, and you can elect a new sheriff.'

'Well now,' the other glanced at Clancy, then looked back at Steve. 'I understood that you'd taken this job for the good of the town, Steve. We can't let you back out now. Could be that somebody else might try to emulate Gruber and we need a man with a gun ready to stop that at the very beginning.'

'But I–' Steve stopped, then grinned. For the first time in a long while, he felt that all of the tension and hatred had been washed out of his mind so that he felt clean and whole again.

Looking up, Steve caught the twinkle in Clancy Tennant's eyes, then turned and he saw that the other's gaze had been on someone behind him. Sarah Tennant stood in the doorway and the smile on her face started the fire in his chest again as he walked slowly towards her.

The publishers hope that this book has given you enjoyable reading. Large Print Books are especially designed to be as easy to see and hold as possible. If you wish a complete list of our books please ask at your local library or write directly to:

Dales Large Print Books
Magna House, Long Preston,
Skipton, North Yorkshire.
BD23 4ND

Other DALES Titles
In Large Print

VICTOR CANNING
The Golden Salamander

HARRY COLE
Policeman's Prelude

ELLIOT CONWAY
The Killing Of El Lobo

SONIA DEANE
Illusion

ANTHONY GILBERT
Murder By Experts

ALANNA KNIGHT
In The Shadow Of The Minster

GEORGES SIMENON
Maigret And The Millionaires

SOLE SURVIVOR

Steve Yarborough was the sole survivor of an attack on a wagon train by a band of renegade outlaws. Struggling to a small ranch on the edge of cattle country, he is nursed back to health by Clancy Tennant and his pretty daughter Sarah. He learns that the outlaws are working hand in hand with the richest and most powerful of the cattle owners. Steve takes on the job of sheriff, with a mission to rid the territory of the outlaws and destroy the power of Bart Gruber, the man behind this wave of terrorism.